DRAGON BLOOD

DRAGON BLOOD

BY

BRUCE WOODS

www.penmorepress.com

Dragon Blood by Bruce Woods
Copyright © 2019 Bruce Woods

6
BISAC Subject Headings:
FIC031020FICTION / Thrillers / Historical
FIC009100 FICTION / Fantasy / Action & Adventure
FIC009070 FICTION / Fantasy / Dark Fantasy

Edited Christine Wozny
Cover Illustration
The Book Cover Whisperer:
ProfessionalBookCoverDesign.com
Address all correspondence to:

Penmore Press LLC
920 N Javelina Pl
Tucson AZ 85748

DEDICATION

For Mary Sonnichsen, Ethan, and Alice

"It's poor judgment," said Grandpa, "to call anything by a name. We don't know what a hobgoblin or a vampire or a troll is. Could be lots of things. You can't heave them into categories with labels and say they'll act one way or another. That'd be silly. They're people. People who do things. Yes, that's the way to put it. People who *do* things."
—Ray Bradbury, *The October Country*

"That war will come is certain."
—G. E. Morrison; Pekin, China; April, 1900

Author's Disclaimer

This is a work of fiction, and the fictional characters herein are, you know, fictional, and not meant to represent anyone living, dead, or undead. If any of them remind you of yourself or someone you know, you have my congratulations or sympathy, depending upon the character involved. It is also a work of historical fiction, however, and much research has gone into accurately representing the times and places portrayed. That said, when an historical personage in this work interacts with a fictional one, the result is of course wholly a figment of my imagination, and not meant to imply how that real individual did, or would, react to vampires, dragons, and other such inconveniences.

As noted, I've gone to some lengths to research the period in which this novel is set, and hope that it will for the most part pass historical muster (saving the Steampunk elements, which, although sometimes quite nifty, are also pure fancy). Dutiful historians will, however, note that in some instances the chronology of the book will intentionally depart from historical accuracy to serve the needs of the story, since the past didn't always occur in the correct order. Any unintentional errors are the fault of the author and not of the various editors who have done so much to give this story whatever charm it might have.

Bruce Woods

Chapter One

In my prior experience the word "china" had been more likely to conjure up images of place settings than of place. Still, when Lady Ellen Terry, ageless *Grande Dame* of the London Theatre and Mistress of the City's Kindred (or what the Fabulous Fiction of the day would call *vampires)* asks a boon, one does not deny it lightly. This applies even more so in my case, since that Lady's patronage had so recently made me quite wealthy. So, though I was in the process of building an existence for myself in the United States when I received her summons, I soon found myself daring the Great Ocean crossing again.

But I must digress. On my first visit I had arrived in England naïve and newly made. Indeed it was the circumstances of that making (and my reaction to it, which caused me no little shame) that had led me to cross the Atlantic in search of some sort of reconciliation with what I had become.

I had, upon arrival, paid my respects to Lady Terry. This formality perhaps represented an excess of caution, but I thought it prudent, given my neonate status. The Mistress received me kindly, offering advice on how to comport myself in her city. Some weeks later, following an apparently chance meeting with the Great Detective Sherlock Holmes, I found myself, at his invitation, in the Sleuth's Baker Street quarters. There I again encountered Lady Terry and she, acting on behalf of the notorious entrepreneur and nation-builder Cecil Rhodes, offered me an opportunity to be of service and to improve, in the process, my expectations dramatically.

The resulting adventure, recounted in an earlier memoire, took me to Africa's Matabeleland, made me rather wealthy and, more importantly, taught me much about my own nature and about the Way of the World. So it was with an enhanced confidence, and no little curiosity, that I responded to her summons.

That invitation did not come immediately however. In fact, it arrived some five years after I had sailed the Atlantic for a second time and established myself in Washington, D.C. There I had obtained an apartment and busied myself with investing my hard-won nest egg. I had learned from Rhodes (and who better to teach one of the algebra, grammar, and theater of finance?) that money in the markets is won on confidence and lost on fear. I did rather well. I was, you can be assured, far less fearful a woman than I had once been. Upon hearing from Lady Ellen, however, I tidied up my American affairs (leaving some financial transactions dangling in a most un-Rhodesian manner) and, with a replying telegram flying ahead of me, I prepared to travel.

I by then considered myself quite an old hand at crossing "The Pond,", so another transit held little to frighten me. One of our ever more advanced modern Steamships reduced the number of days required for that passage, and thus the number of times I was forced to test the growing Enchantment of my eyes in order to earn myself a sup from one of my fellow passengers. In short I arrived in the Old Country in fair form and established myself in Durrant's centrally located and modern "Palace Inn." Once I had registered and made myself presentable, I set off for a meeting that would prove no less propitious and fraught with risk than had my earlier encounter with the Lady of the City, and demonstrate that I still had leagues to travel before I was fully acclimated to the creature I had become.

Having sold my trusty Horace-Wilkershire Coilcycle before my journey back to America years ago, I availed myself of one of the ubiquitous London steam cabs and arrived at the Famous Actress's quarters at the appointed time. Though some years older than when we had first met, she was of course unchanged, and I calculated she could continue her current role for some time yet before "disappearing" and being "reborn" as another Queen of the Stage. The Great Actress received me graciously, offering me tea in the form of an ingénue who, thrilled as she was to be in such company, probably did not require the Enchantment that Lady Terry had placed upon her in order to preserve our secrets.

I supped modestly, too curious to feel any real hunger but unwilling to risk offense by refusing the Mistress of the City's generous offer. Once the girl was dismissed (to remember nothing that her Lady did not wish her to), I sat as bid and, barely able to conceal my eagerness, awaited further elucidation.

"My dear Paulette," she began, "all of Kindred London is still abuzz over your success on the Dark Continent, and I hope to presume upon you yet again by asking you to undertake another errand to a place that is stranger still and no less dangerous."

"There is nothing you could ask of me that I would consider refusing, Ellen," I replied, savoring the familiarity of address that she had granted me half a decade past. "The debts I already owe you would be all but impossible to repay."

"Speak not in haste, my dear," she said, "for the task I have in mind would take you to benighted China, a nation little known to my country's Kin and all aboil in turmoil."

I confess I was somewhat taken aback, but I made a valiant effort to hide any misgivings; though in retrospect I have little doubt that the Lady saw through my dissembling easily.

If she did notice, however, Ellen gave no sign, and continued.

"I believe that nation is at a crossroads," she said. "Its leadership is in disarray, with many of its luminaries lost to sloth or opium, corruption or palace intrigue. The army is no better, as has been proven in every recent conflict. Its ruler, the Dowager Empress Cixi, is by all reports brilliant but cruel and self-centered. Rather than serve the realm, she plots and schemes, using her intelligence for no purpose other than to maintain her grip on power and sate her cravings for pleasure. These, at least, are the opinions of the informants I have relied upon.

"In short, one of the largest and richest lands left on this planet appears helpless, and the Great Powers of the earth jockey with one another, each seeking position to claim the greatest part when the regime tumbles, as most believe it must."

"I confess I knew nothing of all this," I said.

"Few do," Lady Ellen replied, "but it is my belief that the world will soon learn all this and more. A fuse has been lit in the East, and the explosion to come will be heard far and wide."

This little dissertation left me confused and anxious, but I kept an even tone as I answered

"And what is it you would have me do?" I said. The Mistress was in dishabille, her makeup and costume from her most recent part only partially removed, but I believed that I had never seen a woman so beautiful, or so brimming with power.

"When we spoke before your African journey, I believe you referenced the belief that China might hide Kin of ours behind its Great Wall and painted fans. Indeed I once suspected Cixi to be such, but all reports indicate that she is not immune to aging, so whatever sort of creature she is, she is not one of us. Of late, however, rumors tell of others claiming unnatural powers. Because you were so successful in locating our African relatives, I would ask you to look into these tales, and if possible (though it is said to be forbidden) to speak to the Dowager herself, the latter if for nothing else to satisfy my curiosity.

"If it were no more than this," she continued, casting her expressive voice low and intimate (I had to cut my eyes away from her face for fear of Entrancement, for though she looked no older, her glance had gradually gained in force), "I would not ask you to go, but there are other matters, perhaps interconnected, in which I seek your aid.

"As you know, I enjoy what hegemony I do in this land in part because of my willingness to turn to the talents of the Kin in support of Queen and Country when asked, and it is such a task I would beg you to undertake.

"A hot wind is now fanning the flames of racism in China, Paulette. And, like dust in a drought, it has blown up an army. They call themselves "the boxers' society of righteous and harmonious fists," or some variation thereof, and practice rituals that they claim bestow invulnerability and more. There has been no shortage of such delusions in history, of course, including recently the Ghost Dancers of the Paiute in your own country's West. This is a movement of the impoverished, farm boys left helpless by the fickleness of weather, and boatmen and porters made redundant by the Western miracles of railway and telegraph. They are ill-armed and poorly trained but potentially numberless.

"Recently an auxiliary movement has sprung up. Reportedly consisting of young virgin women, from the ages of 12 to 18 and accounted uncommonly beautiful. They carry the name "Red Lanterns," and claim the powers of flight, fire-starting, and miraculous healing. It is these I wish you to investigate for any sign of Kindred activity.

"More to the point, however, and though the Boxers alone present a threat through sheer force of numbers, the Dowager is perched upon a knife edge. Two camps of courtiers vie for her attention, moderates who would have her eliminate the Boxers for fear that, with the foreigners gone, they would turn upon her throne; and conservatives who urge her to throw in her hand with them to rid the Empire off all peoples and technologies from beyond its borders.

"There is a chance, should she choose the latter, that such a cleansing might succeed. Only to be followed by a hurricane of reaction by the World Powers that would destroy Cixi's government and lead to the dismemberment of China and the eventual distribution of its land among those governments participating in her downfall. England would prefer that this not happen, and that a more orderly infiltration of Modern Thought and Trade win the day. If it is of any concern to you, my dear, your own Nation shares that goal.

"Thus the delicate nature of the charges I would lay upon you: Go to China, investigate the claims of these "Lanterns;" and, however many must die in the process, do what you can to assure that the extermination of the foreigners ultimately fails and the Dowager remains in power so the Great Game can proceed apace."

All but overwhelmed by this flood of information, I managed an answer.

"Rhodesia taught me something of the chess matches of nations, Ellen, and that education owed much to your good offices. I will of course do what I can."

"I knew you would choose so, dear girl," the Lady said. "Before you fully commit, however, I must offer you some additional information. First, one of the preferred methods of murder in that land is decapitation, to which even your body is vulnerable. Second, since anti-foreignism is the breeze that feeds this immolation, it would be advisable for you to travel in disguise." (And here she glanced around her room, all acluttter with costume and greasepaint.) "I might be able to offer some assistance in such matters."

"But," I began, wondering how to phrase my concerns, "while hair can be dyed and straightened, and skin painted, how would I manage my eyes, much less my..." and here I let my embarrassed eyes drop to below my waist.

Lady Ellen laughed then, bright and melodious and refreshing.

"I have a plan for your eyes, dear Paulette, and as for your unvoiced concerns, despite the xenophobic rumors to the contrary, the ladies of Asia are made the same as we are in their nether regions."

I confess I would have blushed had I not learned to control that instinct.

"Very well then," I said, "I am in your hands."

Chapter Two

My commitment made, I soon learned that there was an additional difficulty posed by Lady Ellen's plans. Where I had been fortunate to avail myself of the services of a translator in Africa, I was to pose as a local in China. Thus I was set the task of learning Manchurian, the language of the Dowager Empress's people. A Manchu disguise (rather than that of the Chinese *Han* majority) would have the advantage of freeing me from the necessity of feigning foot binding, as that form of torture was practiced more commonly by the Hans and had not been embraced by those of the northern race that now held the throne.

Despite (or perhaps in part because of) my access to translators on my previous journey, I had found languages surprisingly easy to acquire while in Africa, and it seems that this was another gift bestowed upon me by my (all unwilling) making. For though the Manchu tongue is accounted to be passing difficult I was soon pleased by my progress. However, because I cannot assume my readers have had the luxury of such an education, I will present all dialog in this account in English, which, when prudent, I used while narrating the daily events into the Tessier-Ashpool Recording Device I kept secreted within my personal goods during much of the adventure.

My disguise might also merit some words of explanation. In this Lady Terry proved true to her word, combining the magics of stagecraft and Modern Science with the physical advantages bestowed by my Kindred state.

A wig was deemed unworkable, vulnerable as it would be to removal by suspicious hands or dislodgment by my own activities. Fortunately, my blond hair, though curled, had been quite long when I was made (and, as is the way of the Kin, would only grow if cut or otherwise lost, and if so will return to the length it enjoyed upon my turning). It was a small matter for Lady Ellen's *coiffeuses* to straighten my locks (with many a cooing at their beauty and texture) and dye them a midnight blue-black. Unless I was somehow shorn, I would have no need to reapply this coloring.

Styling my crowning glory also presented no challenge to my attendants, though I confess that I found duplicating their efforts at least as daunting as learning the language. Fortunately, I would be posing as a single woman, and thus was spared the more complicated and ferociously decorated buns favored by those who wished to announce to all and sundry that they were wed. In the end we settled upon a single long braid, with silver jewelry embroidered into the tip, and set off with hairpins fashioned of that same precious metal and bedecked with pressed flowers.

The color of my skin needed modification as well, which was accomplished by bathing in a tub, the water of which was infused with exotic herbs and barks. These produced a hue not so much yellow (contrary to the popular Western misconception), but of a gentle honey-tan. I was assured that this would last the course, and that in most instances much of it would be hidden by my clothing. (I said nothing to the latter, though I thought it not unlikely that I would be seen unclothed before the adventure was over.)

My eyes were more problematic. Lady Ellen's creatures solved this difficulty in a most interesting manner. I am not qualified to discuss the surgical roads they took, but was assured of their success.

The final step was one I alone insisted on. Though crude, it was solid enough to charge my confidence, which is the key to disguise: Using a wire no thicker than a cobweb, they took a stitch in the corner of each eye and wove this strand beneath my hair, pulling the tiny cable tightly enough to narrow and slant my gaze. After the initial bite of the needle, my skin rapidly healed around the stitches with no lingering discomfort. The pain was brief, largely because of my nature, and I studied it while it lasted, like a small creature temporarily cupped within my hand. The result was not fully accurate, but Lady Ellen assured me that, given the racial clues presented by my appearance as a whole, this was unlikely to engender suspicion among the anthropologically innocent people I would most often encounter.

Though now slanted, my eyes were still blue (a hue particularly offensive to the Dowager, I was informed, since they reminded her of cats, for which she had an unnatural loathing), and not at all in keeping with my disguise. I first proposed to wear tinted eyeglasses, for which I had developed a liking, but this idea was quickly discarded as such are not common among the Chinese masses and would offer a fragile hide at best.

Ellen then produced the latest wonder of the glass-blower's art, and a clear indication of the miracles continually being generated by the March of Science. These consisted of a pair of fine lenses, each no bigger than the tip of my finger, which were dyed a dark brown/black and could be inserted directly into my eyes. I found the application of these difficult, however, and their presence irritating, and feared for their efficacy in the dust common to the Chinese roads. Eventually we settled upon a liquid which, upon application of a drop into each eye, would produce the appropriate color. This chemical burned sorely upon initial use, but the pain soon ceased and I was told that a single treatment would last several days.

My face was whitened with a clay-like substance, my mouth painted bright and small. The cosmetic effect did not extend to include my neck, and thus took on the appearance of a mask.

I was dressed in a traditional long gown and loose cotton trousers, dark blue to indicate someone of less than grandee or Mandarin class, with a stand-up collar and embroidered with floral designs. Cloth shoes, similarly decorated and with soft soles, and worn over socks of the same color, completed my outward apparel. A sash around the waist, coupled with the gown's voluminous sleeves, provided ample hiding places for the things I might wish to keep concealed. The rest would be wrapped in a simple bedroll.

The transformation accomplished, my Patroness instructed me to take to the streets (while I continued with my language studies) and accustom myself to my new appearance and the reactions it generated; both to become familiar with the costume and to determine where, if anywhere, it required refinement.

I soon found that I was, as can be imagined, quite the object of curiosity, even in this most Cosmopolitan of cities. The wealthier classes did what they could to hide the intensity of their study, and even occasionally favored me with polite bows. Those lower on the economic scale, however, were less considerate. Tradeswomen hissed condemnations behind my back, and men seemed to find my appearance arousing; at least such was indicated by the catcalls of "China doll," and the invitations to participate in increasingly unlikely sexual couplings, that punctuated my perambulations.

My African expedition had done much to show me the rotten wood that often lurks behind the veneer of civilization, and my experiences as a "Chinese maid" in old London Town did nothing to disprove this discovery. Indeed, before I had set foot in the Mysterious East I found myself wondering about the righteousness of my mission, and speculating that one society's enlightenment was another's barbarism.

Misgivings aside, however, within a week I felt truly transformed, and Paulette Monot gave way to Jinyu Liu (the name Lady Ellen had suggested as appropriate for me, upon consultation with those "China hands" of her acquaintance). At this stage, and after I had been disguised for some time, Ellen examined me closely, even parting my hair to determine how well the skin dye had penetrated this barrier. She pronounced herself satisfied, but with a caveat.

"The ingredients I've used here were old, Paulette, and I am concerned about the permanence of the effect. I believe it best if we remove the coloration for now, and that you interrupt your upcoming journey for a brief visit to Delhi, where a friend of mine can supply you with all that will be required to provide a more resilient transformation when you reach your destination. Until then, I fear we must wash away the dye lest it fail in part and leave you piebald."

The removal of my coloration proved to be more painful than its application, consisting as it did of a second bath in a substance that essentially stripped away a layer of skin. I found the experience, and the necessary healing that followed it, left me quite drained, so my host summoned the young actress who had fed me earlier to provide a boost of energy before the stylists repaired what damage the second wash had done to my hair.

Prior to describing my travels, it might be instructive to make note of a few of the items that Lady Terry bade me equip myself with for the final leg of my journey. (It being decided that travelling in masquerade might draw unwelcome attention, and with the ingredients for my skin dye awaiting me in far off India, I would sojourn as a dark-haired, strange-eyed version of myself until near the end of my travels, and only complete my full costume when the soil of the East was under my feet, employing, among other things, a simple hook and loop worked into the wires at the corner of each brow).

I was to take along with me the cunning little pepper-box pistol which had accompanied me to Africa, a lovely thing of brass and ivory, its multiple barrels loaded with cartridges tipped with an amalgam of lead and silver, each with a heart of good English oak. It was thus suitable for putting paid to adversaries of a variety of natures. A small ampoule of eye-drops was also included, as well as two changes of clothing; one duplicating my everyday costume and a second identical but all in crimson, after what was reported to be the fashion of the Red Lanterns whom I had been charged to investigate.

Of course I would also pack my Tessier-Ashpool listening device (how otherwise would I have composed this account?), and a minimal toilette kit in order to clean myself. Lady Ellen cautioned me against using the latter too assiduously, as it seems the peasantry in the land for where I was bound was not as regular as Westerners in their ablutions. (I now suspect the former is more due to the fickle nature of water supplies than to any national lack of hygiene.) A rice bowl and chopsticks (which I was to find useful, as they allowed the appearance of activity without the need to actually consume any solid food) completed this portion of my kit.

As for the luggage that would sustain me until I "went underground," I limited myself to one trunk. Though I was under no illusion that the journey would not be long and wearisome, I knew as well that all things Western would needs be abandoned when I assumed my new identity. Thus I packed lightly (as I have learned to do), but with an eye toward coquetry, as I would have to be responsible for my own dining during my travels.

As before Lady Ellen presided over the logistical components of my journey (though I am sure she had an army of assistants). Perhaps because she worried that I would be weary of ocean travel following my recent Atlantic crossing, she arranged for the bulk of my travel to be by airship or rail, beginning once again with a short jaunt to

Paris on the luxurious airship *Boadicea,* acknowledged queen of the skies.

From there, unfortunately, my accommodations would become less enviable, probably because there was not sufficient passenger traffic to pay for and thus justify the accoutrements of luxury. Instead, the vehicles that carried me hence were supported by trade in freight, and only accommodated such passengers as I as an afterthought. Where I journeyed by rail the cargo was heavy, and usually of coal or some other mineral of value. On the airships, however, weight was ever a concern, and though I was unable to verify it, I assumed that the freight consisted of some substance which carried an inordinate value per pound. Given the state of the world and my (limited) knowledge of recent history, I suspected that I was accompanied into the air by crates of opium.

If such was the case, I saw no signs of indulgence among the (small) crews and (smaller) contingents of passengers. Fortunately even the greatest of these freighters of the air were forced to land at intervals to take in fuel or deliver and pick up goods. I was able to use such brief respites to feed myself, usually without doing any lasting damage to my victims' bodies (though I cannot speak for their minds), and thus avoid the potential for disturbance among the intimate and often tightly knit travelling communities. More traditional meals I would convey to my quarters, as I had done in Africa, and secrete the foodstuffs where I could to give the impression of consuming an acceptable mortal diet.

Thus from London I rode the *Boadicea,* and then sojourned to, in turn, Ankara, Delhi, and Tokyo. In the second of these great cities I disembarked and, with directions in hand and an adventurous spirit to further guide me, set out to find the contact (Lady Ellen assured me that I would be expected) who was to provide me with the ingredients needed to transform my skin from the palest of Occidental whites to an Asian gold.

The Raj, as Britain's Indian protectorate was called, was itself held to be a place of some danger to Westerners, with less than fifty years having passed since the Sepoy Revolt that had so taxed the Empire, and with much of the nation in the grip of a famine no less brutal than that then ravaging China. I detected no hostility in the crowds through which I journeyed, however, and despite my pale skin I wondered if my dark eyes and blue-black tresses perhaps served to confuse my race.

Much of Delhi still showed damage resulting from the Sepoy wars, which occasioned the odd detour, and I was quite surprised by the density of humanity that seemed to seethe and pulse down its every street. This, and the cacophony of sounds and scents, proved a challenge to my heightened senses, accustomed as they had become to the relative lack of stimulation provided by rail and airship travel. Soon enough, however, I found my contact, one Sanjit Chopra, ensconced as Lady Terry had said he would be in a small chemists' establishment within a short bicycle taxi journey (steam being unfortunately slow to follow in the footsteps of the British army) from the aerodrome.

Mr. Chopra, who I identified as Kin immediately, was quite taken with the work done upon my eyes and hair, and insisted upon examining both closely, though I wondered if his enthusiasm was an attempt to spark further intimacy. He was a man of average height, and had clearly been taken in his maturity. He sported a small round belly, black hair combed back and dressed with some sort of fragrant oil, and a pair of gold-rimmed spectacles fitted with what I was quite sure were cosmetic lenses. The gentleman was bedecked in a white *sherwani* jacket worn over matching *churidar* trousers, an outfit not unlike those I would soon encounter in China.

He offered me refreshment, but I had enjoyed a dalliance on the prior leg of my journey and had no need of nourishment. We spent a pleasant half hour nonetheless, he proving to be an *aficionado* of the theater and curious to know all about the upcoming season in London, all the while hovering over me like a doting parent or an amorous squire.

I was unresponsive to his overtures, if that they were and not just an exaggerated politeness, and courteous enough in our exchanges to reflect my neonate status, and in short order he had provided me with a small paper packet and far more detailed instructions than I had need of. I thanked him profusely, promising to give his regards to "the dear Ellen" as he termed her, and was quickly once again on my way.

I confess that aside from this one detour I had little time or inclination to enjoy the exotic climes through which I passed, and was glad when I reached the last of them to finish my disguise and abandon my *portmanteau*. After obtaining lodging and immediately requesting that a hot tub be drawn (to wash the dirt of travel off, or so I claimed), I was soon able to complete my transformation (though I struggled mightily with the face paint and the dressing of my hair) and, leaving my Western belongings behind to benefit, I fear, the landlord and not those in his employ, I emerged onto the streets of Tokyo no longer Paulette Monot but Jinyu

Liu, prepared, with other travelers at the edge of their luck, to take a steamship to the Chinese port of Kingdow.

I had wondered how I might maintain the charade of preparing my meals while ship-bound, but soon discovered that the same cook responsible for feeding the crew was willing to provide rice for passengers for the price of a single copper *quing*, or with the appropriate change from a silver *tael* (these being the coinages in use at the time), or for the exchange of an equivalent amount of dried grain, for a bowl of cooked (sometimes with the added bonus of a few bits of onion or other vegetables). This I would convey to a secluded space, though privacy was difficult to come by in such crowded conditions, and worry at with my chopsticks to give the appearance of eating.

Most of my fellow passengers were Chinese, primarily from the peasant and merchant classes, who had decided to repatriate as a result of the current political scene, in which Japan had proven to be the most dangerous of their nation's foes. I spoke to several, at first attempting to excuse my pronunciation with a claim that I suffered a speech impediment (a ruse I quickly discarded when I discovered there were accents enough in the Cantonese melting pot to explain any of my own verbal idiosyncrasies).

It was here that I heard my initial first-hand accounts of the Society of Righteous and Harmonious Fists, who had come to be known by Westerners and many Chinese alike as simply "the Boxers." They had exploded upon the countryside, and spread rapidly; either because, as Ellen had posited, the recent drought and modernization had left many of the poor without work, or because they offered food (often taken by threat of force from the villages they entered, or stolen or extorted from Chinese Christians) to converts, or because of a widespread belief in the Boxers' abilities to defy bullet and blade, start fires from a distance, or summon an angelic army of ancestors to drive the Foreigners from the home land; or some combination thereof.

Of the Red Lanterns I heard less; indeed there seemed a fundamental difficulty with the existence of such an auxiliary given the Boxers' purported fear of the power of female sexuality, or "yin." It was maintained as factual by them that Westerners, and particularly missionaries, defeated the Society's magic be smearing their Christian faces with menstrual blood, or flying flags woven from female pubic hair atop their churches and cathedrals.

During these conversations with my fellow passengers, some important shortcomings in my disguise came to light. I had just finished eating one evening (or rather pushing my rice about in a parody of such), when a young woman of approximately my apparent age approached and, eyes cast down, politely asked if she might join me. Setting the bowl and chopsticks aside, I patted a place beside me on the crate that served as my perch.

We exchanged names. Hers was Li-hua, which I knew from my studies to mean "beautiful pear blossom." It was not an overstatement.

"You are not eating," she said, with a nod to my bowl. "Are you feeling poorly?"

I shook my head wearily.

"It is the boat," I said. "My stomach seems always a half roll behind, and it turns itself in its efforts to keep up."

Li-hua laughed, a hand to her mouth.

"We will be on land soon," she said, "and then you must eat! If you become too thin the men will not desire you!"

I was not sure how to respond to this, so I tossed my head, my braid swinging.

"Surely that is more their concern than mine." I said.

My companion appeared startled at this, and studied my face before speaking.

"Forgive me!" Li-hua said. "Are you not a courtesan?"

"I am but an unwed girl," I said, feigning outrage, "who has not yet been forced to sell her body to keep rice in her bowl."

"I beg your pardon!" she said, sitting up straight. "I did not think to offend, it is just..." and here she touched her own face and her unbound hair

I am usually quite observant, but now I realized that I had allowed my concerns for the tasks ahead to blind me to my surroundings. My new friend, and indeed most of the Chinese women on our ship, wore her hair loose without adornment and her face free of the clay and paint that masked my own.

I laughed, imitating her own embarrassment.

"Oh!" I said, "I had forgotten that I had done this! An old woman on board had promised that she could make me beautiful for a price, and I was vain enough to allow it. I gave little thought to the fact that it might give the impression that I was advertising my services."

I unbound my hair and removed its decorations, offering the bits of silver and dried flowers to my companion.

"A gift to you," I said, "in thanks for the shame you have saved me."

This Li-hua refused.

"Keep them, please," she said, "you will be able to sell them on land. Such riches are rare these days, and will certainly purchase you food or travel...." She hesitated, cutting a slantindicular glance at my abandoned bowl. "...but if you truly cannot finish your meal, would you be so kind as to allow me to do so?"

I nodded my assent, tucking my chopsticks in my sash (with a resolution to wash them as soon as I had an opportunity) and slid the rice toward her.

She ate hungrily, holding the bowl close to her mouth and using her implements to push the food in, not so much lifting the rice as shoveling it, and managing somehow to continue speaking between swallows.

"You do not need such paint and decoration," Li-hua assured me. "You are very beautiful. In fact, I would find it easier to believe you were a courtesan than that no man has claimed you!"

I sighed, wondering as I did how such a beauty as she had also remained single.

"Perhaps there will be time for marriage someday. The world is too uncertain now, and I believe, simple woman though I am, that I might have a part to play in its unfolding."

Rice finished, Li-hua returned the bowl to me with a nod.

"I fear that there will be many deaths before the future reveals itself, Liu. I wish you happiness, and that your dreams steer you safely through the days ahead. There is a tub of seawater on deck, near the rear stack. Many use it, but it is clean enough to wash your face and your bowl and chopsticks, I think. Perhaps our journeys will allow us to meet again."

With another bow she left me, and I hurried to undertake the ablution she had recommended in order to remove my face paint. I was grateful to have learned this lesson before arriving on land, for who knows the difficulties such a misrepresentation might have brought upon me!

Chapter Three

Kingdow had been a German protectorate since the Dowager conceded it in reparation for the murder of missionaries in Shandong province in 1897. Upon arriving there, I was immediately grateful for Li-hua's advice. For where a courtesan might have attracted attention, I found myself all but invisible to the Western residents of that coastal town. Indeed, there seemed little evidence of the strife I had prepared myself to encounter. I had yet to learn that China is huge and complex, and that peace might be found on one side of a hill and Bedlam on the other.

This coastal town, however, seemed preserved in amber on the calmer side of that mount. Still, I had to make a conscious effort to remember that I did not appear to be a Westerner, lest an innocent greeting to one of the Germans perambulating in his jinrikishaw might be taken for insolence and result in a demand for my punishment. For though the races mingled on Kingdow's streets, there was an invisible border between them, as if the fortunate travelled safe within bubbles; if not unseen, then certainly unaffected by the Chinese chasing a modest income up and down the dusty roadways.

From the gossip on those lanes, however, I soon discovered that I should not have to travel far to discover unrest. Given the vague nature of the mission entrusted to me, I determined that my first objective must be to encounter a band of Boxers, and to hope that, somewhere in their vicinity, the mysterious Red Lanterns might also be located.

I carried nothing but my bedroll, rice bowl, and the other items detailed above; thus even a form of transportation as primitive as the oxcarts with which I had plodded across Africa would, I thought, be perceived as extravagant. So, after a few days in Kingdow, which served to bolster my confidence in both my disguise and language, I set off toward the interior, aiming roughly for the town of Tientsin. The Chinese roads were said to be dangerous, the lurking-grounds of bandit and Boxer and Imperial troopers, one as likely to be bent toward rape and robbery as the other. If their various gods answered their prayers, they would not encounter Jinyu Liu, and, all unknowing, discover that they had instead met Paulette Monot.

With the addition of a conical hat woven of bamboo strips, purchased in town after an appropriate period of haggling, I was well protected against the cruel sunlight. Still, grateful for my augmented night vision, I chose to travel in the dark as often as possible, when my blue clothing would render me all but invisible. I took my rest during the brightest hours in simple inns along the way, where I disposed of my silver trinkets in exchange for lodging and the ubiquitous drought and famine made my refusal to join in what rude meals were on offer altogether unremarkable.

The roads were often raised between croplands, the latter sometimes high with grains that had sprung up after the belated January rains, but which shimmered now in the daily heat. Both road and field would surely be deep in mud should precipitation ever return, an event widely believed by the residents not likely to occur until the foreign devils were, one and all, killed or driven from the land. Signs of poverty and misery were everywhere. I encountered barren trees, which would in better times be heavy with the blossoms that promised sweet fruits, from which the bark had been stripped, presumably to provide flavor to soups that were otherwise no more than hot water.

Fear kept much of the populace from the roads at night. This presented me with a double-edged sword, as it meant that anyone I did meet up with would be unlikely to look benevolently upon a young woman travelling alone. It was not until my third evening, however, that I encountered such unwelcome company. I heard them before I saw them, and of course perceived them before they did me. Rather than attempt to hide in the struggling fields on either side of me, though, I determined to endure the encounter and see what it might teach me.

There were two of them, young men unmarked by either military trappings or the red clothing said to identify the Boxers. They carried no arms that I could perceive other than a small hand-scythe and a pruning knife, which looked imposing despite their innocent agricultural origins. The men smelt of sweat and dust and deprivation, and challenged me as soon as I came within their sight.

"Ho!" said the larger of the two (they might have been brothers, but any such fraternal scent was lost beneath the layers of odor that had accumulated in travel), "don't you know these roads are dangerous after dark?"

"Surely not as hazardous as those behind me," I replied. "My mother and father are dead there, and I hope to find relatives in Tientsin who will shelter me as I seek work."

They fingered their weapons.

"You'll find no employment for such as you in that town," said the speaker. "There is only one thing you have to offer, and why would a man pay for it when he can take it?'

"I am no courtesan," I said, letting my roll slip off my shoulder and showing offense, "You see before you only a daughter of the land, blown as you might be by the winds of misfortune."

They made to grasp my shoulders, pulling their weapons free.

"You will have reason to thank us, then, for we will teach you a marketable skill."

I could have fled, of course, and let my unnatural speed leave them in a superstitious funk, but it had been some time since I'd fed, and I had seen injustice enough already to leave me short of temper. Instead, I stepped back, freeing my clothing from their hands.

"A good man would not threaten such, "I said.

The smaller of the two spoke now, brandishing his knife.

"The good men in China are long dead, girl," he said. "Undress for us and perhaps we will leave you with your clothing and your life. It is as generous as offer as you're likely to find on this road."

I could smell the lust rising in them, triggered as it is in the worst of men by the anticipation of violence.

They grabbed me again, taking my arms in their free hands, and I struggled enough to make their dragging me from the road and into the brittle fields satisfying.

"Make an outcry and I'll cut your throat," hissed the larger, already worrying at his clothes. "And you keep watch," he instructed his companion. "I'll just warm her up for you."

As the smaller stepped back, I shook off the other's grip, as easily as a debutant might shrug a fallen leaf from the naked glory of her shoulder, and crushed his throat with a quick blow from the flat of my hand. The short man gasped and made to run, but he had not taken two steps before I caught the back of his clothing and spun him to face me. Holding him close, I broke his right wrist with one hand and whispered, my mouth close to his own, my voice already lisping around the erection of my feeding teeth.

"And now it is just you and me. It is better when one isn't forced to share, don't you think?"

In the dark his eyes were wide with fear, and his moans low in his throat. I felt his erection go soft as terror unmanned him.

"Do you still want to kiss me?" I asked, showing him my fangs and twisting the broken wrist again so the pain would keep him conscious.

He was quite beyond replying, so I buried my teeth in his dirty neck. His blood was thin, and spiced with terror, and I took what I needed. I could have let him live, but an irrational anger still mastered me, and when I was quite sated I let him drop, picked up his crude blade, and drove it between his eyes. It had all happened so quickly that I fear he had not had time to enjoy the fabled pleasure of the feeding. There were corpses enough along the road, and the packs of curs I'd seen following me at a safe distance would, I was sure, soon enough leave little evidence of the means of his and his companion's passings.

I wish I could better explain the cruelty of my actions. Perhaps my ill humor was simply a result of being immersed in two cultures, each of which thought the other barbarian, while rendering my own judgment on both. I had certainly seen evidence of human foibles, and had yet to even encounter the heart of the tragedy I was charged with exploring. Or, it is also possible that I was just, as they say, "in a mood." At any rate, somewhat refreshed I returned to the road, shouldered my bedroll, and resumed my lonely journey.

Chapter Four

I was not destined to be alone for long, it seems, for shortly thereafter I encountered sights and sounds that bespoke a welcome familiarity. If there is a unique heartbeat to Our Modern Age, it must be the rhythmic muttering of wheel upon rail; and if Scientific Advancement has its own sweet breath, what form could it take but the white billows of a steam engine? I was frankly surprised that, so early in my adventure, such signs of the Civilization I'd left behind were so welcome to me. I hurried forward, eager for this little reunion.

I had of course known that a railroad ran between the cities of Tientsin and Pekin, it being one of the first such signs of Modernization in China, but the barren road and poverty that had so far marked my journey had quite driven the memory from my mind. The trains, when they hove into view, seemed as miraculous to my eyes as some mythological dragon.

They were idling when I finally came upon them, the great steam locomotives motionless but huffing peacefully like creatures at rest, while workers conducted repairs to the tracks ahead. I approached carefully, uncertain of what sort of welcome I might receive. Any concerns I had were quickly dispelled, however. Though the trains fairly bristled with fighting forces representing all of the Great Powers, there were Chinese aplenty as well, fulfilling the myriad roles that keep an army on its feet.

Just as fortuitous, I discovered, as I began to tentatively mingle with these workers, that there was an air of unbridled optimism surrounding the expedition; a confidence that drove paranoia before it and thus made it quite simple for me to insert myself into a crew preparing food for and serving the troops, whose mission soon became clear to me.

The force (though international and thus fractious by nature) was under the nominal leadership of one Vice Admiral Sir Edward Seymour, and had been hastily assembled to travel from Tientsin to Pekin and there provide support to the international Legations should the threats that they were then facing get out of hand. The journey (of only about 100 miles) was expected to be an easy one, little more than a jaunt by rail across the countryside, and soldier and worker alike were in high spirits despite the current delay caused by vandalism to the tracks ahead.

This expedition, consisting of more than 2000 troops representing eight nations (Britain, Germany, Russia, France, America, Japan, Italy, and Austria) was travelling in what could only be called (in wartime at least, though no such conflict had been declared) luxury, with a club car among those that made up the trains and a goodly stock of spirits assigned in lots to individual soldiers and carefully allocated by a dedicated steward.

Whatever misgivings I had about my disguise (particularly in light of the errors Li-hua had pointed out to me on shipboard), were quickly dispelled as well, as I was accepted without question by all and sundry. The disruption to the tracks ahead was quickly made right, and I found myself, rather than slogging alone on a desolate road, riding easily with a merry company and lulled by the peaceful chant of rail travel, though away from Tientsin and toward Pekin.

Rations were adequate for all. The workers assuredly were not treated to the puddings and wine available to the Westerners, but the rice was plentiful and served with good fresh vegetables and enough meat to infuse flavor into the grain. Having so recently fed, of course, I had no need to eat and no appetite for such foodstuffs, but none seemed to take notice of my abstinence as I busied myself with chores and sought to educate myself about recent events through the chatter of my fellow travelers.

Seymour's mission, I learned, had been undertaken in response to the increasingly frantic communications received by the various ships anchored off the Chinese coast, sent from their respective ministers in the capitol. Though the ambitions of the several Powers were widely divergent, the urgency of the summonses eventually lead to compromise and, since the local Chinese Viceroy had approved a movement of troops across Chinese territory to support the Pekin Legations, the risk was seen to be minimal. Indeed, I learned that the trains had only recently passed by a Division of Imperial troops without incident, which had served to further buoy spirits.

Of course my limited understanding of the situation indicated that matters were far more uncertain than this assessment implied. I also felt, however, that the arrival of Seymour's force in Pekin would promote stability and improve the chances that the crisis would be resolved as Lady Ellen wished, with the survival of the Empire and a China open to Western influence, so I resolved to bide my time and observe events.

My first night aboard the trains was a pleasant one. The evening meal was met with approval by one and all, and after it had been enthusiastically discussed the soldiers exchanged patriotic songs of their varied nations in a friendly competition (since the British and German troops enjoyed the greatest numbers, their contributions were certainly louder, if not more melodious, that those of the other nations).

Soon the rattle of the tracks had itself sung most of the revelers to sleep, however, and I was able to roam my train, ostensibly offering service to the few night owls who remained awake. By day our journey had generated a regular audience of onlookers from the villages we passed, the steam engine being still something of a curiosity (if not always a popular one, as it was rumored that the noise of the trains disturbed the rest of the mythological dragons that slumbered beneath the Chinese nation) among the local populace. I was surprised, however, to see the same interest in our passage displayed well into the evening. If any of my companions were able to see such gatherings, however, they, as did I, attached little significance to their presence.

On the following morning, as the trains approached Langfang, roughly halfway between Tientsin and Pekin, we again had to stop in order to repair damage that had been inflicted upon the track ahead. There was some speculation as to who was responsible for this act of vandalism, and whether it might be either simply superstitious villagers or the Boxers themselves. This conundrum, however, was soon answered quite dramatically.

At first I thought the gathering in the fields adjacent to us might be related to some local fair, as there was certainly an air of festivity about it; with much dancing, posturing, and leaping about. It soon became clear, however, that we were facing our first joust against the Boxers. There were some hundreds of them, each wearing either part of all of a uniform of red, including caps, socks, and sashes, with their weapons (mostly swords and spears, which albeit primitive, were nevertheless quite fearsome looking) similarly decorated.

Far from being intimidated by this display, however, the Western troops seemed quite eager to come to first blows with this new enemy. It proved to be a battle unlike any of them had ever experienced.

The initial contact, which I did not learn about until later, was apparently between the rebels and a small squad of five Italian sailors, nominally on picket duty, who were surprised at their tea by a force of Boxers. The return of the rains had done its work here, and maize and millet crops often grew right to the edge of the railroad embankment. These crops had perhaps allowed the Chinese to come upon the Italians unawares, and the Europeans were wiped out to a man, doing little if any damage to their enemy in the process. This was certainly the only victory, if judged by normal military measures, that the Boxers were to enjoy that day.

The traditions of arms, however, had little influence upon the mode of battle employed by our foes. Given their belief in the invulnerability conferred by their rituals, one would not have expected a cautious approach. I was reminded, however, of the epic battles between the colonial forces and their foes in the Metabele war, during which many of the latter also believed themselves to be proof against bullet and blade. I more than once speculated that, had the Boxers been led by one of the African King Lobengula's crafty Impi generals, it might have gone more poorly for Seymour's forces.

Even a simple massed charge, and discipline be damned, would have inflicted significant damage, but nothing was simple to the red-clad warriors. Instead, they would gather at some distance from the train and there go through the rituals that they believed would armor them or even allow them to be possessed by their gods (many of whom were based upon the fictional heroes of the pantos popular in rural fairs). These actions involved much dancing and waving of sashes, until the whole force was perambulating like a ballet choreographed by Beelzebub. While the Boxers indulged in these antics, they provided excellent target practice for Seymour's riflemen and Maxim guns.

The incontrovertible proof of vulnerability provided by these mortalities did not have the expected effect, though. Perhaps the uninjured believed that their fallen comrades had not been righteous enough, or had performed their ceremonies incorrectly, for despite death all around them still they came on.

Often they were able to come entirely too close to closing with the Western troops, though their advances were typically slow and stately, and punctuated by much continued gesticulating and waving of their antique weaponry. Many of those in Seymour's command remarked after the fact that the Boxers were decidedly difficult to bring down, often requiring multiple hits by modern weapons. Whether this was a result of their fanaticism, the inadequacy of the small-bore rifles carried by some Western troops, or simply excitable shooting I leave for other chroniclers to parse out.

I personally observed one gigantic Chinaman, armed with a two-handed sword, advancing ponderously to within yards of the train, while the troops facing him seemed to vacillate between offering fire and seeking the relative safety of the interior of the carriage. Several shots were fired at him, but most were I think directed by panic rather than gun sight, and it was only two pistol bullets as desperately close range that finally brought him to the ground.

Though I had my pepper-box wrapped securely in my sash, I avoided taking part in the battle for fear that questions would arise concerning how one as poor as I might have gotten possession of such a cunning little firearm. Instead I stayed in character and supplied water and ammunition to the troops as waves of Boxers burst out of the crops, first here and then there, all to be met by hails of deadly lead.

On several occasions the attackers did actually manage to get in among the Western troops, and in these instances fierce hand-to-hand fighting was the order of the day, often with bayonet pitched against spear and sword. Eventually, however, superiority of arms, and in particular the use of the automatic Maxim guns, won the day. This again brought to mind the Metabele War, and reminded me of the exceptional dissipating power that weapons firing some 600 rounds per minute had upon an enemy's enthusiasm.

Leaving more than 100 dead behind (it was rumored that the Boxers killed their own wounded to prevent them from falling into the hands of the "terrible barbarians"), the remaining attackers finally slipped back in among the crops and fled, perhaps to fight another day or, with a simple change of clothing, to resume their lives as farmers and tradesmen. As successful as the battle was for the Powers, however, Seymour rightly recognized it as a sign of things to come, and attempted to take appropriate precautions.

His first order of business was to solicit scouts to scour the countryside ahead and perhaps help the command to anticipate future actions. Frustrated to have spent the attack figuratively sitting on my hands (with, I modestly assumed, more battle experience of my own than many of those to whom I had served water), I volunteered for such a role. Seymour was initially hesitant to allow this, due perhaps to some sort of misguided Victorian sense of chivalry, but it being pointed out that, as a member of the softer sex, I would not likely be perceived as a threat to any I might encounter, he reluctantly gave me leave to sally forth.

Prior to venturing out I retrieved my bedroll (the better to appear a simple transient on the road), and reloaded my pepper-box pistol with simple lead-tipped cartridges, there being no need to waste the silver and hardwood bullets on the targets I was likely to acquire. This I tucked into my sash to assure quick access. Thus equipped, I took myself into the crop fields, planning to circle around and ahead of the trains, which were still becalmed while the damaged tracks were being repaired.

Once well out of sight of those of the expedition, I was pleased to enjoy the opportunity to employ one of the talents of the Kin. Though we are not able to render ourselves invisible, contrary to one of the prevalent Myths of the day, we are able to move in such a manner that makes us difficult to perceive to any not knowing precisely what to look for, and I was confident that such knowledge would be quite beyond any mortals that I might encounter. This movement was complicated, however, by the fronds of the crops through which I traveled, which were ever ready to emit a tell-tale rustle at the smallest incautious step.

Perhaps I was guilty of overconfidence, for it was one such careless tread that almost brought me to ruin. A single stalk of maize, perhaps brought down by an animal seeking the succulent kernels higher upon it, lay flat upon the earth. My eyes elsewhere, I stepped directly upon this plant, producing the distinctive crunch that only dried vegetation can generate.

As luck would have it a band of four Boxers had taken shelter in the field nearby. Deciding correctly that only an enemy would be creeping along in such proximity, they burst forth, swords waving, and prepared to bring me low, woman or no.

Slipping my pepper-box free from my sash, I waited until they were almost upon me before bringing three of them down with its four barrels, and noting with some satisfaction that their purported resistance to gunfire did not seem in evidence when the shots were well directed. My pistol empty, and with no time to reload, I fled back the way I had come, reasoning that I was unlikely to encounter additional enemies along that route, with the fourth Boxer in close pursuit.

This situation was of course quite to my liking. Reaching a small clearing, I turned to face him with a snarl, my teeth sprung free from my gums. Faced with an apparition pulled whole from his nightmares, the Boxer dropped his sword and took to his heels. His flight availed him nothing, however, and in three long steps I had wrapped the trailing queue of his pigtail around my fist and quite jerked him off his feet.

Eyes wide, he lay on the ground making the most frantic of gesticulations, presumably willing one of his opera gods to possess him and thus rescue him from impending doom. I waited for some moments, long enough to allow him to realize that no supernatural aid would be in the offing, and then fell upon him, pinning his arms with my own, and buried my teeth in his throat.

I was not famished, but the joy of a feed taken thus by force washed over me, the fear flavored his blood in a most addictive manner, and I reveled in the pleasure of feeding. He was alive when I left him, though weak with blood loss and pleasure, and whether he would be able to recover or would remain where he was to perish of exposure I can only guess.

It took me some little while to master myself, knowing that to run amok among any enemies I might find would, however satisfying, serve no end. So once calmed I returned to my planned patrol. There was, I soon discovered, no shortage of red-clad fighters mustering along the train route ahead of Seymour's force. The villages I encountered, too, were one and all in a high state of excitement, and I suspected many of their residents had Boxer paraphernalia secreted away and ready to be donned when called upon to drive off the foreign devils.

Though I had recharged my pepper-box, I made no effort to engage any of these gatherings, but simply completed a wide sweep of the fields and fallow lands that the trains must cross in the days to come. This reconnoiter convinced me that the prospects for rapid travel by rail were indeed poor, all the more so because a number of the Boxer squads I observed were already in the process of further damaging the rails and ties ahead.

After first taking care to clean myself of any lingering blood, the sap from the stalks of the surrounding crops serving since water was in short supply, I moved quietly until I was in sight of the trains and hurried to make my report to Seymour. I soon discovered that the recent attack had quite changed the dispositions of the Western defenders, and I came very near to being fired upon before I could convince the pickets, in accented and simple English (since fortunately there were some British troops among those confronting me) that I was friend and not foe.

Seymour did not appear surprised by the intelligence I provided him, it only reinforcing the suspicions that had been germinating in his mind as a result of the recent attack. Deciding to err on the side of caution (where his previous missteps, including certainly the hasty nature of his expedition, had taken a decidedly more aggressive turn), he determined to exercise a second precaution and send the trains carrying the French and German troops back along the route they had come. This would allow them to secure an intermediate station and protect communications with

Tientsin and a line of retreat, should that course of action prove necessary.

As a result of this decision I had the opportunity to observe at first hand the difficulties inherent in a multi-national command. For while Seymour was the purported leader of the relief expedition, he had under his orders troops of seven other nations, and the mutual suspicion among these impromptu allies was only exceeded by their mistrust of the Chinese themselves.

So it was that the Vice Admiral's orders were not well received by those in charge of the German and French forces, who suspected Seymour of planning, through this decidedly practical action, to assure that British troops would be the first to arrive in Pekin and relieve the Legations, and thus receive the credit for that accomplishment and all the glory associated with it. After some heated discussion, the Franco-German leaders flatly refused to support their commanding officer's plan.

Chapter Five

It did not take long for the upshots of this international recalcitrance to manifest themselves. In fact the very next morning, when an engine and several cars were dispatched to Tientsin to refresh the expedition's supplies, it was discovered that the rails had been irreparably damaged by the Boxers at a point just beyond the next station. Matters quickly went from bad to worse, and that outpost itself was overrun the following evening, resulting in the destruction of telegraph lines and the cutting of communications between Seymour and his allies fore and aft. Unable to more forward or back by rail, and with no means of providing any with information about its plight, the relief expedition found itself stranded between Tientsin and Pekin.

Thus the Boxers, though they had suffered what can only be called a disastrous military defeat, had accomplished a goal that many would have thought impossible. They had effectively prevented aid from reaching the Delegations in the capitol, and in doing do pushed the nation inexorably closer to a full state of war.

Perhaps emboldened by this success, the enemy forces increased their attacks on Seymour's troops. Despite whatever shortcomings I had noted in their commanders, the warriors had clearly learned a lesson from their earlier defeat as well. As often as not they now either abandoned their posturing or completed such rituals before commencing their attacks, and were occasionally able to make use of the cover provided by crops in the fields to approach closer to the trains before breaking into the open and commencing hostilities.

This change in tactics certainly increased the stress suffered by the Western troops, but superiority of armament still won the day in every instance. The question, however, was how long this could remain the case. With no way to recruit new supplies, Seymour's force was left with finite stores of food and ammunition and an ever-increasing burden of wounded to attend to. It would clearly be unable to survive indefinitely in the no-man's-land it now inhabited.

For the moment, however, the situation was not dire. The food served at mess was less varietal than it had previously been to be sure, and some of the officers groused when, for efficiency, they were made to eat with the enlisted men. Others complained that the steward was at times called from his post in order to help beat off attacks, and thus was unable to equitably distribute the spirits allocated for each man. An attempt to send the leading train forward proved futile, however, as the advance was harried by Boxers and hamstrung by broken tracks. When this last effort resulted in failure, the Western commanders were forced to view their situation with hard eyes and come up with a plan of action, however desperate, that might provide them a chance for escape.

I confess I had developed some feeling of loyalty to the expedition. It is remarkable how one can cling to the familiar, and all the more fiercely so when the surroundings are alien. Still, it was clear to me that I was presently doing nothing to propel my mission forward. Thus on the following evening I slipped away from the trains quite as easily as I had originally joined them and set my feet back toward Tientsin to better understand the situation in that city and the capitol.

I had no encounters of any sort for some time, though I could often hear the noise of distant conflicts carrying on the still, dry air, and another pack of mongrels contrived to shadow me at a distance, perhaps thinking my vulnerability would offer them a chance to obtain flesh untainted by putrefaction. On the second night, bored with travel and eager to make an end of it, I continued my perambulations past sunrise and came upon an unlikely apparition.

At first, while at a distance and with fog still burning off the road, I took it for a mule or ox-wagon, but coming closer I found myself approached by be a simple two-wheeled push cart with a middle-aged Western man trudging between the poles. The bed was piled with sundry materials, all crudely bagged or wrapped in bedding. Two woman plodded in its wake, the dust at their feet already defeating the faint dew. The older, who I presumed to be the carter's wife, carried a child of perhaps two or three, and the other appeared to be a maid in her late teens or early twenties. The four looked unspeakably weary, as if momentum was the only lash still driving them.

Such was their exhaustion that I was quite close before they even noticed me. Upon doing so, the man set down the cart poles and pulled a staff from the bed, preparing to defend his family. Holding his stave across his chest, he spoke in the most authoritative voice he could muster.

"Halt," he called out in Manchu, "and declare your intentions!"

I could tell at once that he was no warrior, and answered him in English. In truth I found that producing an accent in this my native tongue was more difficult to master than Chinese itself, but the members of this little party were far beyond noticing any faults in my diction.

"I am naught but a Christian girl, on the road like you," I said.

"If so you travel not from danger but toward it," he replied.

"Perhaps I might join you then, and we might find greater safety in our numbers?"

He muttered something under his breath, presumably to the effect that another woman would add nothing to their strength and further strain their already small rations, but his wife (or so I assumed she was) spoke up.

"We cannot turn away another lamb, Isaac," she said, "not when we have already lost so many."

He acquiesced, albeit begrudgingly, so I took up a place behind the cart and engaged the two women in conversation. They were, as I had guessed, missionaries, in flight from a small church some ten *li* (a unit of measure approximating a third of an English mile) ahead. They had there been set upon by a mob of Boxers, the building burned and their dozens of converts either killed, recanted, or fled.

The wife was named Dorothy and their daughter Belle. Both were dressed in rough cotton and crude, heavy broughams, as unwomanly an attire as could be imagined. It was easy to see how some rural Chinese suspected that the missionary women were in fact men, so disguised in order to steal the eyes and hearts from children for use in their Western magic; though at closer inspection even this genderless attire could not fully disguise the daughter's lush bloom of womanhood.

Before the harsh sun rose too high, we found a path leading away from the road, and hid the cart as well as possible. There Isaac built a small fire, the gathering of fuel for which I fear consumed nearly as much energy as a meal might provide, and cooked a poor breakfast. Unrolling my blanket, I produced my own stock of rice and dried beef, adding some to the communal pot. This brightened the mood of my companions significantly, and so intent were they upon eating that they failed to notice my lack of appetite.

Our meal done and the little fire extinguished, we rested through the heat of the day, I alongside Belle in the poor shade provided by the cart. Those close quarters served to reinforce my perceptions of her femininity, and I found her proximity not at all unpleasant. I resolved to accompany then for some way, to learn what I could and perhaps improve their chances of escape while furthering the missions with which Lady Ellen had charged me. In short, I had a plan.

Our small group moved slowly, the handcart reducing our pace to half that I had been able to maintain on my own.

Once, I was able to perceive a group of men approaching us from in front, and do so early enough to allow us to again quit the road and seek shelter. I found it curious that my companions did not see fit to comment upon my superior vision. Perhaps they attributed it to their own fatigue; or it might have been symptomatic of the misunderstandings that persist between divergent races, and they simply believed that my dark eyes were more animal-like, and thus acute, that their pale ones. This did superstition plague both sides of the nation's brewing conflict.

Just before we were ready to bivouac on the second morning we were approached by a larger group, with no shelter in sight save the croplands that would clearly tell the tale of our entry, and I determined to put my strategy into action. That these were Boxers I had little doubt, as all were bedecked with the red shirts and sashes that identified them as such. Their party consisted of about a dozen men, apparently all in their teens or early twenties. They seemed surprised to encounter us, so I took advantage of their hesitation and stepped in front of the missionary family.

"Please," I said, polite but matter of fact, "Is this the way to Pekin?"

The murmured briefly among themselves before one of the group stepped forward, lifting a crude sword.

"Do you dare to speak for the foreign devils, girl?" he said.

"I speak for myself," I said, tossing my head impatiently. "And these are no devils, just a family as you might find in your own village."

"What insolence!" he said. "Are you a secondary devil that you speak so, and place yourself between the foreigners and justice?"

"If by 'secondary devil' you mean a Chinese Christian, then yes I am. I have heard the Word of Christ." Out of the corner of my eye I saw Belle staring at me with wonder, and tried to quiet her with a small wave of my hand. As I had hoped, the swordsman stepped forward and grabbed me roughly by my arm.

"Then let us see the power of this magical Word, devil," he hissed. "I give you a choice. Recant and come with us and the other hairies go free. Refuse and we will kill you all."

I hesitated, as if in thought, and looked again at the Westerners. As I did so I thought I saw a light of comprehension in the girl's eyes. After an appropriate time I let my face collapse and fell to my knees.

"Spare me!" I cried. "I was never truly one of them. I was starving and the church offered food."

"You will have the chance to deny them more formally in our camp," the Boxer said, jerking me to my feet. "And you," he raised his chin at my companions, "I made a promise and I shall keep it. Off with you, and pray to your false god that I never see you on the soil of China again."

Removing my roll from the cart and leaving it in the dirt, the missionaries moved quickly past me and down the road, the father favoring me with a glance that mixed pity and disgust. Soon the dust of their passage quite obscured them.

I stooped to pick up my bag just before a hand in the middle of my back propelled me ahead.

"Walk," the Boxer said, "and know that I would be grateful for an excuse to leave your worthless body here."

The time, it seemed, for repartee was over. I stepped forward, unsteady as if in fear, anticipating at every moment the sudden bite of the blade.

That steely kiss never came, though I could feel the itching in its owner's hand with every step we took. The trip was only about six lis, but we were well into the heat of the day before it reached an end, and I had ample reason to be grateful for my conical hat.

I knew we were nearing the the Boxer camp before it actually came into view, as I detected a smoky tang on the calm, hot air. The cause of this soon became clear. They had established their stronghold in a small village, now empty of all but the red-garbed fighters. At its center stood the still-smoldering ruins of a little church, perhaps the very one that Belle and her family had fled, giving testimony to the recent violence. Of the former inhabitants I saw no living sign; apparently they had all fled, or in the case of the Chinese Christians either renounced their new religion or been put to the sword, or both.

There seemed to be no national hierarchy to the Boxer organization, with each village or group of such under the leadership of whatever strong man had brought the movement to that place. In this camp the role was played by a small, thin individual with the uncommonly focused eyes of the fanatic, and it was he whom my captors delivered me to.

"Brother disciple Bao," the sword wielder said, forcing me to my knees again (and the reader will likely be able to guess how difficult it was for me to continue to tolerate such treatment without response), "we captured this secondary devil on the road. She claims to have been only a rice Christian. What would you have us do with her?" The commander studied me closely, and then yanked back on my hair to force my eyes to his.

"What is your name girl, and what do you have to say for yourself?" he demanded.

"I am called Jinyu Liu sir," I replied, with what I hoped was suitable meekness. "I am an orphan and was starving. The foreign devils offered me food if I would convert. Words mean little when the cries of the stomach drown them out, and so I did what they asked in order to preserve my life."

Bao laughed. It was a horrible sound, held only on thin reins and threatening to run off into the endless bray of madness.

"She who lies once to save her life will do so again when it is threatened anew," he said. "How should we trust what you say now?"

"If you cannot hear the truth in my words, I beg you to put me to some test," I said.

He laughed his strange hyena laugh again. Behind it, I could imagine him worrying over scenarios. He was loath to admit that he could not magically tell veracity from falsehood, and yet feared as much reaching the wrong conclusion. The opportunity to toy with me provided a useful compromise, and this won the day.

"We could have asked you to kill a secondary devil yourself," he said. "But alas none of their heads have stayed atop their bodies." He turned to enjoy the laughter of his fellows, then seemed to think for a moment, before disappearing into one of the village huts and returning with a crude wooden crucifix in his hands.

"Here, Jinyu Liu," he said, holding the crude wooden cross toward me, "the Westerners place great faith in such rubbish. If you wish to prove yourself uncorrupted by them, urinate upon it."

I snatched the crucifix from his hands, perhaps a bit more rapidly than he expected.

"I am a maiden," I said, the lie coming easily, "and will not shame the memory of my family by doing such in front of a group of men! This, however, will I do."

Symbols meant little to me. If a religion's vision was so narrow as to not include room for the Kin, then I felt I could justly exclude it in turn. I spat upon the relic, snapped it in two, and flung it to the dusty and bloodstained ground.

There was a joint exhalation from the group behind me, a soft and sibilant "Ahhhhh."

"So," Bao said, "you are perhaps not our enemy. But how will you prove your allegiance lies with us? Perhaps the answer hides beneath your garments."

Hands grasped my shoulders again (it was becoming quite tiresome), and I sensed the situation rapidly spiraling out of control. My options seemed limited: fight or flight, and thus risk revealing my nature; or acquiesce, and resign myself to enduring the limited future options of a camp follower. The decision, however, was not to be mine to make.

"So eager to pollute yourself with yin, are you, Brother-disciple Bao?" The voice came from beyond my peripheral vision, but I recognized it immediately. "That will be the downfall of the Boxers, I fear, if my sisters cannot nudge you toward purity."

Those who had grasped me released my clothing as if burned, and I turned my head to face my rescuer. She was dressed in red from head to toe, and carried a lantern in one hand and a crimson fan in the other. She stood tall before me, and stern as a temple god.

"Li-hua!" I said, with no need to feign my surprise.

"Once again I am called upon to save you from a life of sensual degradation, Liu," she replied. "Why is it, I wonder, that fate continually contrives to bring us together so?"

Seemingly infuriated by this exchange, and the loss of face it carried with it, Bao spoke out.

"She is Boxer business, not yours, red witch. If you want her, show us proof of the healing magic you claim!" With this he pulled a knife from his sash and plunged it into my side.

The pain was real; my cry of hurt and surprise and anger no less so.

I fell to the ground and rolled onto my uninjured side, my eyes on Li-hua's, feeding faith to help her combat the doubt I saw flickering there.

She hesitated a moment, and then knelt beside me. At a word from her another red-clad woman emerged at a run from a nearby hut with a pot of steaming water and a rag. The men standing near stepped back simultaneously in the face of this assertion of female control.

Gently but firmly, Li-hua worked my gown up to reveal the gaped wound in my side (the trousers beneath protecting most of my modesty). Using the scrap of cloth provided by the other Red Lantern, she cleaned the surface around the gash, which I hoped no one but I noticed had already nearly stopped bleeding.

Li-hua glanced at my eyes again, and I dared gift her with a tiny reassuring nod. She placed her hands over my cut and, lids closed, lifted her face to the great ball of the sun (which, though my stab wound was by now rapidly healing beneath the covering palms, was making my exposed flesh uncomfortably hot). After a moment she lifted her fan and waved it vigorously, wafting air across the cut which her free hand still covered. She then guided my fingers to replace hers, careful to not expose the gash as she did so, and stood on uneasy knees.

"A Red Lantern has cured her, and the light of the Lantern has marked her," she said softly. There was false bravado in her voice, as there might be in any prayer that despairs of an answer.

As if on cue I removed my hand from the wound. The edges had rejoined, and though the flesh around them was still pink and slick, there was no question that I had been healed.

Bao took one look, eyes grim, and turned on his heel to stalk away. The rest of the Boxers gasped as if struck before following him, whispering nervously among themselves. Li-hua herself did not speak until they were well away, perhaps she was unable to, and even then regarded me curiously before doing so.

"How did you know I could mend you?" she asked.

"I had faith," I said. "It was enough to know you have a good heart, and I have heard tales of the magic of the Red

Lanterns. It is an honor to have provided such proof of that blessing."

"There is no magic greater than faith, and without faith there is no magic," Li-hua spoke as if reciting from rote. "Come dear Liu, let us get you into shelter from the hot sun, and I will tell you what I can of the Red Lanterns. It seems that you might be destined to join us, and perhaps will prove to be one of the weapons we need to kill all the foreigners and to make the churches burn."

The inside of the hut was dark and cool, as clay structures tend to be in all but the most demonic heat. Li-hua led me to rest on the brick kang bed-stove. This was itself chilly, the fire that warmed it and provided heat for cooking having long since been allowed to burn out. She offered me water, which I made as if to sip briefly, claiming that the wounding had left my stomach uncertain, and she proceeded to tell me her tale.

Li-hua had been born into a village in Shandong province. Her mother and father worked the land, and when the rains fell reliably her young life had been a good one, not poisoned by luxury and yet free from any real want. As the years passed, however, her childhood utopia began to wither.

The rains became erratic. It was as if the weather itself were raging in anger, irrationally lashing out first one way and then another. Floods ravaged her home, driving people from their huts and then retreating to leave foul-smelling mud and destruction in their wake. These gave way to drought. Crops that germinated withered in the fields, while others never rose above the brick-hard earth. It was only during the recent January that rains had provided some respite, but by then she and many like her had already taken to the road.

Missionaries, whose governments forced concessions from the cowed Dynasty, built churches willy-nilly, with no thought to the careful feng shui of the areas they invaded. They sought converts, the so-called secondary devils. Some of these were good men and woman engaged in spiritual search, but others were bandits and reprobates, who called upon the protection of the Western Powers to forgive their crimes and thus preyed upon their neighbors with impunity.

In the wake of the churches came steam-engines and telegraph wires, each of which idled thousands in a society where public transport, freight, and communications had formerly been dependent upon the strength of individual limbs and backs. Li-hua was a girl, and thus not a participant in the discussions of men, but she had overheard her father and brothers and cousins, and knew that the fickle weather was believed to be brought on by the alien churches and technologies. The Chinese dragons suffered as a result of these insults, and their agonies were reflected in the river, earth, and skies.

It is true that some of the foreign devils were meek and unobtrusive, seeking to earn converts by good example alone. Others were more aggressive, disrupting the fairs that were the social lifeblood of the villages, and lambasting what they saw as heathenism, promising eternal damnation to those who did not see the error of their benighted ways.

Perhaps, secluded in their privileged enclaves, these men of God did not see that Hell had already opened up all around them.

Li-hua's village was then like many others; its residents starving and, in their hearts, believing that somehow the West, with its missionaries and its machines, was responsible for their misfortune. Thus when the first somewhat ragtag troupe of Boxers arrived, its members were greeted with enthusiasm and found no shortage of adherents. This was not surprising, since they brought entertainment to the idle and, with their ritual and ceremony, the promise of invulnerability to the powerless.

When the missionaries attempted to turn to the authority of the Qing to champion their converts in civil disagreements, they found that the new Society offered an effective buffer against the authority of the state. The local Boxers' reputation grew before Li-hua's eyes, and soon they were actively harassing what they called the secondary devils, and using the food and fortunes they took from these enemies as further motivation to those who would join their ranks.

One of the planks upon which the Society's mythology rested, however, was a demand for sexual purity, and the belief that "female power," referred to as the yin, was the only force that could thwart the Boxers' rituals. This had the two-pronged effect of preventing women from joining their ranks and creating a standing force of young men, now reasonably well fed and active, who struggled with abstinence and sometimes vented their frustration upon female Chinese converts, or even those whom the Boxers could conveniently accuse of being such. Thus Li-hua, and other young women in the villages, found their freedom restricted rather than expanded under the Boxer influence.

The Red Lanterns were perhaps the village girls' response to these developments, a sort of female answer to the Society that also, perhaps, served as a constant reminder to the men to keep to the straight and narrow. Rumored to be virginal and clad all in red, the women had rituals of their own, and at various times claimed the abilities of magical healing, flight, fire-starting, and halting the progress of bullets with a wave of their crimson fans (and even catching the spent projectiles in baskets like so much threshed grain).

Li-hua had joined their ranks early, and, though there was no clear overall leadership in either Society (each group as I've said being either village or regionally based and independent of the others), became a Sister-disciple and noteworthy among these warrior witches. She had, she explained to me, been returning from a self-assigned mission that involved spying upon Japan, among the most feared of China's enemies, when I met her, but (and this she confessed in a whisper, her lips close to my ear) the magic feats of the Lanterns continued to elude her, and she had never before been able to effect a healing as miraculous as that she had just achieved with me.

I stayed some days in the village, supposedly to allow myself to continue to recover, though I of course needed no such recuperation. My lingering, whatever its reason, did permit Li-hua to milk what fame she could from my "miraculous" healing. We slept together upon the kang in her hut, and I determined, based upon her closeness in sleep and the stolen touches she allowed herself while awake, that the Lanterns (or at least my companion) suffered as much from their imposed chastity as did any of the Boxers.

There were no more than a dozen of the woman-warriors in her group, and I was unable to find among them any signs of Kindred ability, or any other supernatural powers for that matter. (I also found them to be representative of the population, rather than the remarkable and virginal young beauties of legend, but attributed the latter characterization to simple romanticism.) So when Li-hua asked me if I would be willing to travel to Tientsin, where apparently the rebels, male and female, had gathered in force to bring about a siege of that city (and where the supernatural Lanterns, if any there were, would surely be), I of course agreed.

It was decided that I would travel with an escort of two of Li-hua's group, to provide me with support on the road (and with the added benefit of these women surely spreading tales of my friend's recent medical triumph). My sponsor also provided me with a short sleeved red top and matching tight trousers to identify me as a member of the Society. The outfit was quite attractive compared to the usual peasant garb, and I surmised that this factor alone must have made the Society appealing to some young women. I of course did not mention the clothing in my roll, which was red but hardly matched the unique cut of the Lantern outfit, for fear of inviting suspicion. I resolved to rid myself of these tell-tale garments at the earliest convenience, and soon was able to do so.

I was allowed some moments of privacy in the hut in order to change my blouse and trousers, and took advantage of this solitude to refresh the eye drops that facilitated my disguise. Li-hua soon joined me there to wish me well, and when she moved to embrace me in farewell I made so bold as to kiss her full on the mouth. She was obviously startled by this, but did not break away, and eventually returned the kiss is the awkward manner of one who has never before indulged in such pleasure. I found her inexperience titillating, and held her quite close for a lingering moment before breaking free with a conspiratorial smile.

My escorts were clearly eager to be heading to Tientsin, where they were sure the combined might of Boxer and Red Lantern would quickly overpower the foreign devils there who had been besieged since soon after Seymour's expedition had departed. They chatted happily as we walked along, and clearly regarded me as a bit of a celebrity as a result of the miracle in which I had participated. The Lanterns preferred to travel in daylight, and I for the most part followed them quietly, my conical hat tilted to protect my face and my arms held close beneath its shade as they were no longer shielded due to the short sleeves of my red gown.

We encountered few people on the road. Among these were families fleeing Tientsin. Some, apparently Christian converts, abandoned the path to hide in the sun-worried fields around us. My companions made no effort to pursue these, but merely fluttered their fans in the direction of the refugees, an act which caused one couple to cover their children with their bodies and wail piteously.

Each day as evening approached we watched for roadside inns. I never saw a single silver tael change hands at these establishments, and assumed that providing free lodging to such as us was seen as the better part of valor. I was thankful, whatever the reason, for the luxury of occasionally having a room of my own (this apparently a bow to my celebrity, my companions typically shared their quarters) in order to whisper into my Recording Device and, when called for, attend to the details of my disguise.

As we neared the Hai River we began to encounter crowds, largely of Boxers but with small groups of Red Lanterns in evidence as well. From speaking with the latter, my companions learned that the outer barricade of the walled city was soon to be breached, and many churches would surely be burned and secondary devils either killed or forced to flee. This news was received with excitement, and we redoubled our pace to reach the site of the ongoing siege.

I was able to smell the battle far before we saw it. Corpses, primarily of Chinese Christians but including a few unlucky Boxers as well, had been allowed to remain where they fell in the chaos, and the pitiless sun had stewed this flesh into a miasma of corruption that had to be breathed to be believed. In the closing miles we became inured to the site of dogs and stray swine fighting over bodies beside the road. In fact, my escorts clapped their hands and cooed with delight at these, as excited as if the horror were nothing more than a staged entertainment in one of their summer fairs.

In the distance we could also see long columns of Imperial troops, easily distinguishable in their orderly muster from the continuously dispersing and coalescing mobs of the Boxers. My companions noted these, and wondered aloud what the Qing might do, but were secure in their belief in magic and seemed to consider the better trained and better armed soldiers no particular threat.

As we reached the edge of the city, we heard innumerable tales of the prowess of the Lanterns, who were variously credited with igniting churches from afar and rendering useless the guns of the foreigners, both troops and civilians alike. (There were rumored to be more than 2,000 of the former protecting the nearly 700 merchants and missionaries, and their untold numbers of Chinese servants, in a separate fortified foreign settlement within the soon to be breached outer mud walls.) I was able to verify none of these miraculous deeds, though, and began to fear that the first portion of my mission would come to naught. However, nothing was to prove as simple as it seemed.

Chapter Six

My companions and I spent that first Tientsin night with a group of several dozen Red Lanterns. We camped far enough behind the constantly moving Boxer lines to avoid any gender-inspired conflicts, and the clear skies and warm temperatures made for comfortable camping for those bedded down around me.

The complex of Tientsin was surrounded by a low mud wall. Within this barrier were the fortress-like walled Chinese city itself and the foreign concessions, which were also protected by walls and hastily constructed barricades that had sprung up following the approach of the Boxers. As dawn broke on June 15th the milling red-clad armies ahead of us suddenly coalesced (as a flock of birds will all at once become of one mind, shape itself and veer all together), and swarmed the low outer barricade.

The invaders were not particularly well armed, but the citizens within the wall were even less so, and in the ensuing panic few made any effort to defend themselves. The foreigners, soldiers or no, who were equipped with modern weapons were content to hold their positions within their keep, only spending precious ammunition when the pursuing Boxers drove their victims too close to that redoubt. It was a recipe for slaughter, and no other outcome was likely.

If the Chinese Christians were targeted, then it seemed that anyone not wearing red was branded a convert. The Boxers attacked indiscriminately, often pausing in their rampage to repeatedly slash or chop at corpses already fallen to their brothers' blades. The smell of blood was thick upon the air, overpowering even the stench of bodies killed before. It was only with an effort of will that I resisted it and kept my hidden nature from revealing itself.

I held back from the center of the action, momentarily allying myself with a group of young Red Lanterns. There was little healing to be done save of the occasional Boxer who had accidentally run afoul of one of his compatriots in a killing frenzy, and the care-giving I saw performed by my erstwhile sisters involved nothing more than rudimentary first aid and the crudest of folk medicines. In short, any of the wounded who would needs rely upon magic to make them whole were unlikely to ever rise again from the Tientsin earth.

As the nightmare expanded around me, a swelling cry caught my attention, as much moan as cheer, and I turned to see the first of a group of churches leap into flame, its boards dry as kindling under the steady sun. If there were any Christians seeking shelter inside, they did not exit, as the doors were barricaded from without. Even in the bright light of the day we could feel the furnace-blast of heat from the conflagration. My companions and I stepped back from it, though the Boxers near at hand seemed to feel nothing (I suspected some of them would wake upon the morrow and wonder where their eyebrows had gone!)

My hat was shielding my face, but something other than the light of the fire caused me to turn away. I am not particularly sensitive to human suffering, but the madness of the crowd affected me at a purely animal level. Nothing and no one, my instincts seems to scream to me, was safe here. There may be something on this earth more frightening than a mob, but if so I was grateful that I had not yet encountered it. The Lanterns did not share my discomfort, though, and watched the flames with an almost narcotized fascination.

So when *they* began shrieking and pointing to the sky, thin arms flailing with excitement, I turned again, against my better judgment and a primitive reptilian-brain sense of self preservation, and followed their pointing hands. Just before the second church ignited, fire climbing it as if the building had been lathered in oil, I saw an impossibility.

Dancing atop the flames, fully thirty feet above the earth, was a woman in red; and the blaze seemed to sway to the frantic rhythm of her fans. There was, I suddenly decided, something more terrifying than a mob after all.

Chapter Seven

I was quite beside myself with confusion and excitement. Turning, I grabbed the nearest Lantern and shook her.

"Who is she? What is her name? I demanded.

The girl did not answer, but only stood, open mouthed in superstitious wonder, and stared at the woman above the flames. I repeated my interrogation to another, and yet another, but all were rapt at this proof of the powers of their Society, powers to which each believed she could someday aspire. It was apparent that future queries of this group would provide me with no answers. Turning, with a hurried glance at the figure hovering above the conflagration, I looked for other sources of information.

It seemed that there was nowhere to turn but to the Boxers themselves. Steeling myself, I pushed forward into the crowd, my former fears of the mob seeming small and unworthy in the face of the ongoing miracle. Unfortunately these warriors were as mesmerized as their female counterparts, and one after another only glanced at me in seeming incomprehension before returning their adoring eyes to the air above the church.

I finally approached the Boxer who seemed to be the leader in this sector, based solely on the evidence of the number of bodies scattered around him.

"The Red Lantern in the fire, who is she?" I demanded. He regarded me stupidly, like a dog commanded to perform an unfamiliar trick.

"Her name! Who is she?" I screamed, shaking him with, had he had his wits about him, he might have sensed was far more force than the slight woman I appeared to be should command.

He blinked, and looked back at me, tearing his eyes away from the fire with difficulty.

"She is Senior Sister-disciple Huo," he said, "the greatest of the Lanterns, more powerful even than the Yellow Lotus Huanglian shengmu."

"Huo." I confirmed. "Thank you. I must speak to her. How can I speak to her?"

The lout favored me with a sly smile, his voice distant as if sifted through hypnosis or some other enchantment.

"She will not come down until the fires have died," he said.

At that point the woman called Huo let out a screech, high-pitched and joyous and victorious. Her voice seemed to cut through the stupor of those below. The Boxers returned to their deadly work with a new enthusiasm, and even some of the earthbound Red Lanterns picked up weapons littering the field and joined in the slaying, their victims as demoralized by the woman in the flames as the killers were inspired. I once again became cognizant of the risk to my own safely, and fled beyond the border of the killing grounds. As I did so the gasp of a sudden up-rush of air told me that another Church had ignited. It seemed like I would have quite a long wait.

In a surprisingly short time, however, the mob ran out of victims, and the game of hacking at corpses proved too tame to hold its interest for long. It was dusk by then, and the lowering fires of the burnt buildings cast a flickering red glow on the scene, creating an image that might have inspired the bard Alighieri's darkest visions. A number of the Boxers glanced hungrily at the fortified foreign compound, but their bloodlust seemed for the moment sated. Soon small cooking fires glimmered into light, some of them within mere feet of the day's harvest of corpses, and a blanket of quiet settled over the living and dead alike.

An hour later and the churches were nothing but coals, winking their red eyes in the smoky darkness. I once again made my way through bodies and Boxers then, snores rising like the grunting of discordant frogs all around me. It took some time (I was careful, as I could not predict what one of these men might do if accidentally awakened from sleep), but eventually I found the brute who had spoken to me before and prepared to nudge him awake with the toe of my shoe, ready to leap back if the need arose.

I was stopped by a finger laid gently upon my elbow, and turned to face a woman. She was smaller than she had appeared when in the sky, clad in the brightest of Lantern red, and her smooth face appeared clay-painted as mine had accidentally been, save that instead of snow white hers was the pale gray of wood ash. Her voice was child-like, bright as a bothering of tiny silver bells. The sound of such girlish tones coming from whatever she might be (because I immediately had no doubt that I was in the presence of great age) frightened me more than had her unexpected touch.

"You were looking for me," she said, raising a crimson fan to cover her mouth and tittering behind it. "Is it possible that you were wishing to make my acquaintance?"

Before I could answer, the creature leaned in close, her breath sweet as wood smoke, and whispered behind her fan.

"I know what you are, you know." She said.

I was more frightened than I would care to admit, and the subject she raised was not one I wished to discuss in company, no matter how soft our whispers and how reassuring the snores of our neighbors. Without a word, then, I turned and walked to an open space near the breached mud wall, not knowing if she would follow or if I would be struck down between one step and the next. Trail after me she did, however, and when we were more safely alone she repeated her statement, punctuated by delighted giggles.

"I know what you are." Huo said again.

I studied her before replying. There was no obvious heat coming off of her, or at least none greater than one would expect from a mortal woman, and her appearance, save the ashy pallor of her skin, was human as well. And yet there was an overwhelming sense of *wrongness* about her. It seemed that my best option was to play for time.

"I am nothing so very rare in this place, I think," I said, "only an orphan girl and more recently a Red Lantern."

Huo flirted behind her fan, and a fancied I could see flames flickering in her dark eyes, though I might have been tricked by the reflections of the now-distant cooking fires.

"Please don't take me for a fool, blood-sucker," she simpered. "I'm in such a pleasant mood, and I'd hate to disrupt it with anger. Especially so with you all alone and so very far from home."

Desperate, I attempted to use my nascent powers of Enchantment, but whatever force they might have had merely ran off her dark eyes like water on window glass. I dropped my gaze before she could take further offense, and spoke the helpless truth.

"And I have no inkling of what you are, Huo." I said.

"Ah, so now we can begin," the creature, whatever she might be, favored me with a smile, and despite myself I felt a childish pleasure at that gift. "But my name is not really Huo, it is Lady Zhurong, or perhaps Zhulong; or maybe it is Yaoquai or T'an-mo. So many names! I seldom, refer to myself, you see, and thus all of my appellations are those given to me by these," she waved a fan at the sleeping mob before us with an almost maternal gentleness.

"I could be a demon, or a spirit of this land; anything but a dragon, no, that would be another kettle of scales entirely. I was here before the humans, and so they have explained me. Mankind, the beast that knows little and makes up stories to help it understand the rest! But each new tale dilutes the former, doesn't it? Hmmm. Perhaps then you should call me Huo after all?"

"I don't understand..." I began.

She fanned herself in a show of impatience.

"Of course you don't! Why not make up a fiction to comfort yourself? Surely you are human enough still for that."

I decided not to rise to this bait.

"And yet you claim to know what I am," I said.

"Of course! I may be old but I've lost few of my senses, I hope," she said. "You will be surprised to know that your Kind can be found not far from here, on the little island of the Qing's enemies. But not in China, no, I've made quite certain of that!"

Here at last was information that I could use.

"Do you mean in Japan, that creatures such as I can be found there? And if there, why not here?'

"So many questions!" She seemed quite exasperated. "I see you are still far more human that you might like to admit. Yes, yes, there is a nest or two of blood-suckers in Japan, as you call it. You might even encounter them some day if you survive so long. But the Middle Kingdom has been isolated, inviolate since first the humans appeared. Oh, a few of your Kind have come, braving the waters, but those I have killed or driven off."

I tensed at this revelation, and at the threat that lurked within it.

"And why have you done so, Huo; certainly they were no danger to you."

"To me?" She laughed again, somehow both coy and dismissive. "Of course they posed no threat to me! But the flower that is treasured most blooms alone. I would not have their magic, however small, detract from the glory of mine."

Helplessness was a feeling alien to me, indeed it had been generally so even before my making, but I felt it now, and voiced the question I most dreaded.

"Do you mean me harm then, Huo?"

She peered at me over the edge of her fan, black eyes twinkling.

"Oh, I think not, not yet at least," she said. "You are a visitor, for the most part well behaved, and I would not anger your Mistress needlessly. If you leave when your dance is done and do nothing to recklessly anger me I will allow you to go unharmed. Be warned though, should you beget any here and they remain behind, they will not long survive your departure."

"That I have no intention of doing," I said, and preceded as if reading a catechism, "there are rules...."

"Rules!" she interrupted with a dramatic sigh. "If they were not often broken there would be no need of them! You have my promise, and if you are wiser than your years you will not test it. Now, why did you ask about me?"

I dearly wished to flee, but somehow knew that flight would avail me little. Better, rather, to hold fast and learn what I might.

"I wonder why you've come to the aid of these humans," I said, with a glance to the sleeping bodies littering the ground. "Surely you do not choose a side in such a purely mortal contest?"

"I take pleasure in fire," she said, "but when it is larger than the spark in the kang or the twinkle in a cooking ring, the humans fear it and struggle against it. It is seldom that I have been cheered on for great burnings, and I find it a pleasant novelty. It has awakened in me a penchant for destruction that I have decided to nurture. Besides, I rather enjoy this form," she traced the curves of her body with her spread fans. "You find it comely do you not?"

She was indeed beautiful, pallor and all, but there was a taint to her loveliness, as when one first leans in to kiss a handsome lover and is met with the stink of rotten teeth within the shapely mouth.

"So this is not your true form?" I asked, delicately avoiding the question of her form's physical appeal.

Huo laughed, the sound of it as pretty and delicate as the first lilies-of-the-valley of spring.

"This? Heavens no! When in my true state the mountains are the nine nubs of my spine, the still lakes my eyes, the clouds in the heavens my breath... or is that what the dragons claim? You see how confusing it all becomes? It's enough for you to know that I can take many shapes as they suit my purpose. This one does me nicely for now."

I was about to question Huo further when a disturbance broke out. The first light of dawn was upon us, and its low sun seemed to settle like dew upon the scenes of horror all around. We heard the cracking of repeated small arms fire; something that had not played a part in the previous day's massacre. The Boxers were generally not equipped with firearms, and when they were it was with the most ancient and cumbersome weapons imaginable.

In the rising light I could easily make out a little family group, consisting of parents and an infant, huddled in the narrow alleyway between two unburned huts. They were presumably Chinese Christians (though to be honest all non-

Boxers found in the area the day before had been assumed such) who had miraculously escaped the slaughter thus far.

The gunfire came from a group of Western men who had crept out of the barricaded foreign settlements apparently bent on rescue. Since the Boxers had been for the most part asleep, and awoke to confusion and gunfire, they were not at their most effective. Still, many of them did rush at the Europeans, perhaps confident in their supposed invulnerability, only to be cut down in short order. The little rescue succeeded, and by the time it was over the red-clad rebels were awake one and all, and itching for a fight.

After much hurried and excited talking (during which it occurred to me again that the lack of a central leadership structure and not their paucity of generals was perhaps the greatest weakness of the Boxers) it was decided that the Western settlements must be destroyed. Perhaps overconfident as a result of the prior day's butchering, the mob eschewed any strategy and attacked *en masse*, a horde of screaming men (this group was mostly male, the Red Lanterns having resumed their largely medicinal role) waving bladed weapons.

Many were summarily shot dead. The Westerners obviously expected some sort of retaliation for the rescue and were prepared. They seemed, as well, to be proficient marksmen, though the massed attack of the Boxers did not present them with particularly difficult targets.

I had watched Huo during this debacle, searching for any sign of sympathy for the warriors whom she had seemed to champion just hours ago, but saw nothing on her lovely face save curiosity and a sprinkling of disdain.

"Aren't you going to help them, then?" I asked. "Surely there are buildings within the foreign enclave that you could burn? The Boxer I spoke to said you were greater even than the legendary Red Lantern called Yellow Lotus Huanglian shengmu."

She stretched, fans folded, and stood, as if surprised to have been sitting so long and in need of a good limbering. Her voice when she deigned to speak was impatient.

"Greater than that harlot and charlatan? I should hope so. But to come when they call me, oh that would not do at all," she said. "Were I to intercede during their every hour of need they would come to think that they controlled me. Look, the poor things already suffer from their delusions of infallibility, it would be cruel for me to add to that vulnerability." She smiled sweetly to me as she said this, and I sensed that avoiding cruelty was not high among her motivations.

"You mentioned my Mistress," I began, hoping to drop the question while her mind was elsewhere.

Huo looked at me pityingly.

"Are all of your ploys so shallow, girl?" She asked. "As a glance at the newly fallen bodies decorating the field in front of us will testify, ignorance is among the deadliest of diseases. Thus I remain here in the Middle Kingdom but I study the world, as your Mistress hides behind her greasepaint and examines it as well. I know of her and she knows of me, though it is unlikely that we will ever meet. I suspect you are here primarily to reinforce that which she already believes."

She held up her hand to hush me before I could speak, and, flicking open a fan with a shake of her wrist, pointed off beyond the breached wall. A slow heartbeat of percussion music marked the spot where the Imperial forces were again assembling, but still playing no part in the struggles. A few of the Boxers noticed this as well, and screamed catcalls at the distant troops, who were largely obscured by lingering smoke and a thin morning fog.

The army seemed to awaken like a snake, slowly stirring as the warmth of the day reached it. I am no prodigy at the art of estimating large numbers, but there were surely more than 10,000 of them, equipped with field guns and modern weapons. Should the Qing decide to take a side, the results would, I thought, bode poorly for the opposition. The Boxers seemed to recognize this, and I noted that despite their shouted insults their banners had been amended to read "support the Qing, kill all the foreigners," the first phrase a new addition and quite contrary to their original revolutionary aims.

Thus the day progressed, with the Boxers employing various crude strategies and unable to make any real headway against the barricaded and rifle-bristling foreign settlements, and the Imperial troops drilling in the distance. Huo seemed content for the nons to remain in my company, perhaps only to assure herself that I did not venture off alone without sufficiently admiring her. For my part I was glad enough to listen to her conversations and sift through them for whatever nuggets she might let slip.

At one point, far into the following evening (neither of us had slept or eaten, though in truth I knew not how she took in nourishment), I asked her if she could assist me in obtaining an audience with the Empress Dowager. The question seemed to delight her, presenting as it did another opportunity to point out my naiveté.

"It would be quite impossible!" she said, "at least it would be so for any but me. She sees almost no one, and has only recently allowed herself to be viewed by some from the embassies in an attempt to appear "modern". Why ever would you seek to do so, though? She is crafty for a mortal, and you are unlikely to learn anything she does not wish you to, and what she wants you to learn will benefit only her."

"Are you quite sure she is human?" I asked.

Huo sniffed elegantly.

"By the bags beneath her eyes and the flat sacks of her breasts, I assure you that she is thoroughly mortal, and already rotting from within as they do."

As she spoke the first sliver of sun tore the edge of the horizon. We had talked through the last hours of the night, and this time with the spreading light came the hollow booming of artillery. It was June 17, and the Imperial army had apparently chosen a side.

Huo smiled at me.

"How fortunate for you, my little Red Lantern," she said. "It appears the Venerable Hag might be willing to see you after all!"

CHAPTER EIGHT

"You speak as if you despise her," I said, surprised at Huo's venomous depiction of the Dowager Empress.

"No, in truth she has been a friend to the Kingdom, and defended it with ferocity, for all that I care about such things. Rather I pity her, for her abilities are constantly countered by her human frailties. I suspect the pain of self-knowledge will kill her before any assassin can. But perhaps not before your audience?"

Despite the urgency implied by Huo's words, we lingered there for some hours. I eventually grew hungry and fed upon the wounded without hesitation, little caring if my needs hastened their ends, as there was nothing Huo would learn of me from that activity. If she obtained nutrition at all it was from fire, and she did indulge in small burnings on occasion, though nothing that would change the course of the battle. Each time she did so the Boxers took heart; though their numbers were ever less; as the crops germinated in the January rains, though stunted by the more recent drought, matured and called the rural poor back to the harvest. The passage of Chinese artillery shells overhead was constant, however, and such that I would have expected the foreign quarters to be reduced to rubble and splinters, but this was not so.

Huo provided the explanation.

"Gunpowder and the other components used in the manufacture of artillery shells are quite valuable, and munitions plant workers are poorly paid for dangerous labor." She told me. "No one is surprised that they pilfer here and there and sell what they can on the black market. After all, few in the Qing expected these weapons to ever be used!"

Another shell sailed overhead, and landed with a meaty "crump" but no explosion, punctuating her statement.

"You said the Dowager would see me now," I said in the brief quiet between bombardments. "Why do you think so?"

"The troops are shelling the Westerners," she replied with a pout indicating her displeasure at my stupidity. "Poor Cixi has allied herself with the uprising and declared war on the whole world. It is like a goat threatening a tiger. She has no choice but to be friendly to her little Boxers and Lanterns now."

"There are fewer of them every day," I said. "If their time has passed they can be of little use to the Qing."

"Ah," the creature simpered, "but the rains that have matured the crops here still elude the north. It is from there that the uprising spreads now, and those it seduces come not here but to the capitol."

In the distance a force of Imperial troops and Boxers again attempted an assault on the compound, and once more were beaten back, leaving brightly clad corpses in their wake.

"I fear the entertainment here grows stale," said Huo, standing and brushing off the seat of her snug red trousers before turning it toward me to inspect for any lingering dirt, not without a coy wiggle. "There will be more Western troops on the way, and the Empire will find that they can neither capture the settlements nor, ultimately, defend their own walled city here. There are fires to be set in Pekin still, where the endgame will surely take place, and a meeting with Cixi to arrange." She sighed dramatically. "If only you could fly, little Liu, this would all be ever so much more convenient."

"Can you not carry me then?" I asked, growing a little impatient with her posturing.

"Appearances dear, appearances!" Huo said. "If I were seen doing so it would be viewed as proof that not all Red Lanterns can fly! One must never reveal chinks in the current mythology, don't you see?"

As we squabbled a limping form approached us. As it drew nearer I recognized Bao, the Boxer leader who had threatened me days ago, and noted with no little satisfaction that he had received gunshot wounds in his right leg and shoulder, though he somehow managed to remain upright.

"Senior Sister-disciple Huo!" he cried out, dropping to one knee and striking his forehead on the ground, "please take to the skies. Our enemies grow bolder as the ashes cool."

She eyed him pityingly.

"Return to your farm, Bao." She said. "The crops need harvesting and your father is too old to do so on his own. The churches are burned and most of the secondary devils dead or fled. You've done more than you could have hoped for here. Leave the rest of the battle to the Qing troops. Go while you still have hopes to live long enough to have grandchildren to regale with lies about your valor!"

I could not resist a jibe of my own, glancing at his wounds with a raised eyebrow.

"I see you've discovered that invulnerability can be a fickle mistress," I said.

He stared at me with hatred.

"It is the yin of the foreign devils!" he said. "They enhance their walls with the dirty blood of women. We were foolish to believe that the Red Lanterns would protect us."

I sighed, and glanced at Huo knowingly. "So it is as it ever was; when men fail the fault is with women. Let us away to Pekin as you suggest. Perhaps there are warriors there still. I fear all we have left here are farm boys with broken dreams."

Bao started to respond, but turned without speaking and stumbled off, shedding his red clothing as he went. Soon he was only in his loincloth; and it was a skinny, crippled man who hobbled off into the distance, a far cry from the frightening figure he had once presented.

Huo shook her head sadly.

"It appears your bard was correct, clothes do make the man," she said. "But we have lingered long enough; it is time we were off."

She approached a group of Red Lanterns nearby who were discussing Bao's departure in excited chatter. A few words from Huo and one of them dropped to her knees, striking her forehead on the earth quite forcefully. Another word, and the creature stood with the woman's spear, decorated with red tassels, in her hand. This she passed to me.

"I have decided that you must travel on your own," she said. "I cannot bear the pace that you must be held to."

I studied the weapon, lifting it to test its weight and balance.

"Surely you know that, even alone, I will have little need for this sort of armament," I said.

She rolled her dark eyes.

"Appearances, appearances. Have you learned nothing from me? If you make haste you will not be too long upon the road. When you arrive I will find you and facilitate your audience. Oh, and there might be another waiting there who will be pleased to see you; your friend, Sister-disciple Li-hua?" The creature leered at me lasciviously, and I was reminded that one of the names she had bandied about translated roughly as "lust."

Fortunately, blushing was something I could control.

"It would be very good to see her again," I said, trying for nonchalance.

"Then be off with you," she said, unfurling her fans and rising into the air. "Every step will bring you closer to her!"

Her ascension did not go unnoticed. Soon all of the Boxers and Lanterns near at hand were exclaiming and raising their hands to point at the sky, only to moan their disappointment as she floated off into the distance. I suspect it was Huo's departure, more than the ripening crops or the guns of the Westerners, which ultimately broke the backs of Tientsin's attackers.

Not knowing what else to do, I slung my bedroll over my shoulder and, spear in hand, set off on the road to Pekin. For the first few lis I had company in the form of small groups of men and women who were once probably Boxers and Lanterns but whom, their red clothing discarded, could no longer be identified as such. They one and all gave me a wide berth, perhaps out of shame that I still wore the tell-tale garb that they had stripped away. Their numbers grew steadily fewer as I progressed, though, and very soon I was alone with the heat, the nodding roadside crops, and the corpses

The temperatures at the height of day were deadly, and I resumed my practice of travelling chiefly at night, at which time I was able to exert the speed of the Kin, and finding morning shelter beneath the overhanging stalks of grain in the roadside fields. Though the heat was little reduced in such crawl-holes, at least I was shielded from the direct sun. I occasionally heard voices while so hidden, but my days passed unmolested.

During the first evening's journey I passed the town of Beicang on the banks of the Hai River. I perceived much military activity in the vicinity, and ranks of Imperial troops establishing positions there in anticipation of any future movement of Western forces hoping to relieve the now siege-bound international delegations in Pekin. Few of the soldiers were actually upon the road, however, and those whom I did meet seemed to consider my scarlet clothing and tasseled spear to be all the credentials required. There might have been as many as 10,000 troops in the town's environs, and it certainly looked like the intended to make things warm for any army attempting to pass.

At some point I must have come near Seymour's trains, though since I often kept well off the path of road and rail I failed to note their position or condition. The activities of the Chinese troops I encountered seemed to be focused upon providing resistance to a force moving from Tientsin toward Pekin, though whether this indicated that the relief trains were no more or had escaped their isolation I could not determine.

I was only challenged once, in the pre-morning darkness as I was considering where to take my daily leisure. I suspect that the poor visibility prevented my assailant from seeing my crimson costume before it was too late; or perhaps he imagined I was carrying plunder from Tientsin, and simple greed got the better of his loyalty to the recent alliance between the Empire and the Lanterns and Boxers.

"Are you a friend of the Qing?" He asked, covering me with his rifle.

I stopped, leaning on my spear.

"The Lanterns are pledged to support the Empire and kill the foreigners," I said, "as are you."

"Indeed," he said, his barrel not wavering. "But looting is not allowed. Will you let me examine your belongings?"

I made no move to drop my roll. Perhaps it was my frustration at not being able to influence the creature Huo that inspired my next action. At any rate I threw all of the strength I had into my eyes, and locked them upon his. I could feel him struggle with the Domination, confused and frightened, and then his rifle lowered until it was facing the ground.

"You will remember nothing of this," I whispered, stepping closer to him. Gently I pushed the firearm aside, and allowed myself a moment to savor his trembling before I took his queue in my free hand and pulled his head back. The poor man was shaking like a patient in a fit of ague by then, but his shivering abruptly ceased when my teeth slipped through the sweat-slickened skin of his neck.

The feeding was as ever an intensely sexual experience, and I pulled him as tightly as a lover against me, sucking greedily until I smelled the spill of his seed. I left him there upon the road, dropped to his knees, to wake and wonder at his unexplained weakness, and at the sticky wetness between his legs.

Fed, I felt flush with energy, but was still compelled to hide from the heat of the day. I moved quickly after waking at the first touch of evening, though, and put miles behind me, careless of any who might wonder at the rush of red along the dusty and heat-baked length of road.

Chapter Nine

As I passed Yangcun and continued on my way, the troops of the Empire were rarely out of my sight. They seemed to be engaged in building fortifications and strategic positions around that town, perhaps to serve as fallback positions should they be unable to hold Beicang. From all directions came the sounds of shovels and picks plied against the baked ground.

I was not approached again, and, being sated, did not seek out any contact. Though the temperatures fell after nightfall (and they were certainly often above 100 degrees in the heat of the day) many insects persisted. These were undoubtedly attracted by the corpses still common along the way, or bred in the stagnant by-waters of the river Hai. I was not bothered by the pests, however, save for the occasional hoards of midges that hovered around me as close as a loose cloak. For some reason that I've never heard explained the insects that most mirror our dietary habits seem not attracted to the Kin.

The low thunder of distant cannon fire provided my introduction to the capitol city. The nearer I drew the greater the crowds became, with Boxers and Lanterns (many I expect newly minted) hurrying toward the town as eager as theater aficionados racing to an opening, and refugees or the wounded struggling against the current of humanity to move in the other direction. Occasionally these two streams would merge and fighting would break out, but by and large the desire to get into or out of the city overrode the urge for such conflicts.

None paid me any special attention, though to be sure the men and women fleeing the city often gave me a wide berth. As I entered the streets of Pekin I was confronted with scenes of horror that quite surpassed any I had encountered thus far. Corpses were everywhere, some piled in a willy-nilly effort at sanitation, but most resting where they fell, and fermenting under the daily heat.

The bodies were joined on the narrow roads by rotting vegetables, dead animals (some of which, including dogs and ponies, had been hurriedly and partially butchered by the hungry inhabitants) and human waste of all kinds. Smells that would quite overpower a mortal nose usually had little impact upon me, but I found myself missing the longer sleeves of my earlier garb, which I could have held up to my face to provide relief of a sort.

With no clear instructions as to where I was to meet Huo, I wandered aimlessly. The streets were indeed filled with Boxers, perhaps more than I had encountered in Tientsin, parading and posturing with arrogant confidence. Here and there lay the bodies of Chinese women, some in a state of partial undress indicating that their attackers had surrendered to the call of yin before (or after) putting their victims to the sword. Of the Red Lanterns I saw little sign. Those that I did encounter tended to travel in small groups and apart from the mobs of men, worrying perhaps that even their fearsome reputation would not be an adequate chastity belt in the face of such unfocused male aggression.

I was not molested, however, though it may have been as much due to the spear I still carried as to any lingering self control on the part of the crowd. As Huo had predicted, the Boxer army was under the loose charge of the Imperial troops, though there seemed to be little strategy and less control inherent in that arrangement.

This became more apparent as I neared the foreign Enclaves, where Western diplomats had barricaded themselves against attack. Here the Boxers kept up a worrying pressure, careless of the bodies that they left on the field with each assault, while the Imperial troops kept out of easy range of the defenders' firearms and poured rifle and cannon shot at the enclave, the latter of which was answered sporadically by a few large guns within.

Once again I was perplexed by the apparent lack of damage done by this fusillade. The walls of the enclave were pocked with the marks of bullet and shell, to be sure, but for the most part they stood, and where significant damage had been done makeshift repairs had restored a modicum of protection. It seemed, at the moment, a stalemate, but with the ranks of Boxers and of more disciplined troops swelling daily, surely the huddled diplomats would be starved out or overrun before too very long. If I were to accomplish the second aim of the mission which Ellen had entrusted to me, something would have to be done.

The walls of the Imperial City complex, close at hand to the legation quarter, were well protected with Qing troops, yet the Boxers seemed to come and go through these lines with impunity. Curious, I followed a raucous group through the army cordon and was surprised to discover that my passage was neither impeded nor questioned. It was as if the Dowager Empress, having tacitly allied her Empire with the Boxers, was increasingly at a loss as to how to control her new friends. The red-clad peasants had, without a struggle, gained access to areas from which their fathers would have been driven at sword point only days ago.

Even these, of course, were forcibly denied entrance to the great main forecourt of the Forbidden City itself, which even Cixi (being, though Empress, only a woman) could not access. Curious, I made my way down a long alleyway and discovered a separate entrance to the inner sanctum, at the end of a passageway surrounded by high walls. It was a dreary passage, but I found that even here the ubiquitous Boxers had made their way and gained entrance. The door ajar, I slipped in to a world of opulence the likes of which I had never encountered.

Therein, the invading peasants behaved as might be expected, wondering at the richness surrounding them and, when not observed, secreting away whatever examples of it that might fit beneath their clothing. It occurred to me that the Dynasty was in every bit as great a peril from the Boxers as were the Western diplomats trapped in their walled Legations.

I was considering intercepting a particularly dirty ruffian who was in the process of stuffing a white jade dish in the shape of an opening lily into his trousers (I am no champion of private property, but I do believe that age is due a certain respect), when I once again felt the touch of a fingertip on my elbow.

"In five minutes he will attempt to purloin another, and in the process shatter both. One can only hope he does himself a lasting injury as a result. But you, my little false Red Lantern, have other flowers to cultivate today."

At the sound of her voice the looter scurried away, knock-kneed as the sharper edges of the jade figure worried at him beneath his clothes.

"I did not see you there, Huo," I whispered, turning to face her.

"Of course you did not, my pretty monster," she said. "I did not wish you to until I was quite ready." Her lovely, ashen face clenched as if she'd caught a wisp of foul air.

"You have recently fed, I see," she said. "And left this one living! There may be hope for you still. These," and here she sniffed disdainfully at the invading Boxers, "simply do not yet know that they are already dead. It is at least one failing of which I cannot accuse you."

"Are your insults the price for the favor I've asked?" I said.

"So sensitive!" She replied. "It is I suppose the prerogative of youth? No, you shall have what you ask. I only hope your wishes are wise in this case, and do not lead you to disappointment or worse."

As we spoke the Boxers had drifted away to further theft, only to be replaced by a tall man in elaborately embroidered robes and a matching serving-bowl of a hat. Huo approached him and they whispered together, heads bowed close. She glanced my way and his dark eyes followed, his face expressionless. Finally he nodded, and approached me, his cloth slippers noiseless on the stone floor.

"Will you kowtow before her?" He asked, his voice surprisingly childlike from such an imposing form. I decided that he must be one of the palace eunuchs, known for being, if not the power behind the throne, at least the facilitators who allowed its complex and prescribed mechanisms to function.

"How should I not in the presence of the Empress Dowager?" I replied, though not averting my eyes from his, as befitting a petitioner in the presence of a mere palace functionary.

He was silent for a moment and I briefly feared that he would not answer at all but remain there speechless and immobile until I was forced to somehow break the impasse. Huo, however, shattered the moment with an impatient flick of her fan.

The eunuch flinched as it slapped, though the expression on his face remained unchanged.

"The Lady will see you," he said, and walked away. With a final glance at my patron, who favored me with an enigmatic smile, I could do nothing but follow.

He proceeded through the chambers, oblivious it seemed to my presence and to the occasional jibe ("oh look, a dog with no tail, a wasp with no sting!") directed at him by the Boxers present. (It is perhaps worth mentioning that they only taunted him from a distance.) We soon left these interlopers behind, however, and the eunuch stopped before a final door.

He raised his hands to me, and I stiffened, fearing some sort of assault, but as I stood firm he only gently touched my hair, removing the more unsightly of its tangles. When he was apparently content that I was as presentable as he could make me, he opened the door and stood to one side.

The entryway led into into a hall, and I immediately perceived a woman at the far side of it. She was seated behind a long table, a scepter at her side. Knowing this could be none other than the Dowager Empress, I dropped to my knees and struck my forehead upon the floor with enough force to produce a satisfactory "thunk" but not sufficient to generate a bruise.

"You may approach," she said, her voice soft and gentle, not at all the tyrannical bark I had expected, and melodic enough to belie her age.

With another (and less aggressive) touch of my head to the paving stones, I stood and walked forward. It was indeed Cixi who welcomed me, and despite her voice she looked every month of her sixty-five years. Her clothing and makeup, however, indicated the care for one's appearance and, yes, the vanity of a younger woman. It seemed the Empress Dowager did battle with the passing years with every bit as much relentless ferocity as she employed in her struggles with her enemies foreign and domestic.

I stopped some two yards in front of her, unsure of the protocol of approaching nearer, and allowed her quick, intelligent eyes to study me. This she did for some moments, with surprising results.

"What name will you go by," she said. And when I had answered, giving my name as Jinyu Liu and saying that she could call me Liu if it pleased her, she waved her hand dismissively, jeweled protectors shielding the two fingernails that she wore long.

"That is no more your name than you are a simple Red Lantern," she said. "You are also not of the same ilk as your champion Huo, I can see that much. So tell me what you are and what you wish to accomplish in this audience. And let me caution you, should you mean me harm I am even now not without my defenses."

It was a complicated series of questions, and I was attempting to craft an answer when the door flew open behind me. This was clearly unanticipated as the Empress almost came out of her seat in surprise. A bizarre apparition gamboled through the entryway, shutting the door upon the eunuch who grasped in futility after it. The man wore the clothes of a Mandarin or grandee, but had slipped over them the red short-sleeved shirt and sash of a Boxer.

I could not initially tell if he was actually mad or only wished to lure madness to himself by so portraying it, but he capered and pranced in a crude parody of the pugilistic formulae that gave the Boxers their name. The Empress clearly recognized the individual, but had never seen him before either in this garb or so possessed. Risking a peripheral glance at her, I clearly saw the impact of this performance upon Cixi. It was as if she were a woman supported by a dozen threads, and was witnessing the unraveling of one of them.

After the fact I was unsure if I had acted upon an opportunity to improve my standing or merely out of impatience, as it was obvious that my audience could not advance while the pseudo Boxer dominated the room with his nonsense. Whether his madness was real or feigned, however, I saw an opportunity to play upon it, and so I did so.

Drawing myself up to my full height (which was at least average in this land), I fixed the play-actor with a hard glare and flicked my fan open.

"You dare disturb the Old Buddha when she is engaged in official Red Lantern business?" I demanded, following the question with a single emphatic flick of the fan.

He attempted to stutter an answer, but I overrode him.

"You dare to mock the Boxers with your antics, as if that will save your head when the time comes?" I fanned the air once again, as if it would blow him out the door.

The grandee was whimpering now, beneath my gaze and the Dowager's, who was herself staring daggers at him. I cut him off a third time.

"You dare pollute this chamber? Perhaps you are a secondary devil seeking a coward's reprieve. Shall I have the true Boxers examine you under their spells to see if you carry the cross on your forehead?" A third flick of the fan was too much for him, and he stumbled out through the door, slamming it closed behind himself.

With no little satisfaction, I drew the accordioned paper closed and slipped the fan into my sash, feeling the Dowager's eyes on me all the while. She had, of course, asked a question, and as an Empress was accustomed to being answered regardless of the interruption. She waited.

"I am, I am a mystery, my Lady," I began, not sure what I intended to say but aware that obfuscation would make me no friend in this room. "I come from England but am not English. I am like nothing you have seen here and, when I have departed, which I hope soon to do, nothing you are likely to see again. I am no enemy to the Qing and no ally to the creature that calls herself Huo. I am an observer, perhaps, riding her curiosity to this world before it changes course and blows me elsewhere."

She tented her hands, the jeweled finger-guards clicking softly as she thought.

"A pretty answer," she allowed, "which weaves a basket of words that contains nothing of substance. The creature that now calls herself Huo came to me in another form," and here the Dowager glanced around, clearly nervous, as if that entity might be listening in even now, "and convinced me to throw in with the uprising, promising me an army that might save my Empire from the Western Powers. I did so, entrusting the Qing to the people of China, only to find that I had traded one enemy for another."

I bowed my head, thinking rapidly as I did.

"Whatever Huo might be," I said, "she has come to Pekin, abandoning the siege of Tientsin. Even now the Boxers melt away there, returning to their homes, and the barricaded Westerners grow in confidence and begin to turn their eyes to the capitol and the relief of the Enclaves here."

"Do you have the second sight, then, you who call yourself Jinyu Liu? Will the Powers take this city, and carve my China like a market pig?"

"I have only the vision of one who's eyes are unclouded, Empress," I said, feeling my way carefully. "The eight nations now allied against you are too strong and too proud to allow failure here. Seymour's forces will eventually make their way back to Tientsin, and the walled city there will fall to them without the support of Huo's fires. Meanwhile the creature will enflame the Boxers here in the capitol. Even now their posters promising the death of all foreigners in three months are pasted over your own edicts banning their sect."

"What choice had I?" she demanded, as if I had charged her for an explanation for this change of course, and I saw a glimpse of the iron will that had allowed this woman to control a great nation for decades, despite the rise and fall of Emperors (often at her hands) and the machinations of rivals who sought to steal her throne.

"China is weak, her navy destroyed by the Japanese and her army stretched thin and wavering in the face of the barbarians. What can I turn to in this hour but the hearts and minds of the people to save my country?" Frustration and fear, the latter obviously an unwelcome emotion in the heart of she who had triumphed time and again over terrible odds, were clearly driving her patience before them like leaves tossed by the biting autumn wind.

I thought rapidly. I knew that the Enclave must not fall, for should their diplomats be slaughtered nothing could keep the Powers from overwhelming the nation and either driving Cixi from power or killing her outright. Either scenario would lead to the partition of China and doom my mission to failure.

"You must look to the sky," I began, dissembling madly. "The enemy is not within the Western barricades, but above. It is the reason your forces failed in Tientsin and will do so here. The foreigners have called upon their own spirit army to counter the magic of the Boxers and defend the Enclaves. Only by firing into the sky over their shelters can your forces keep the ghosts at bay and achieve victory."

The Empress studied me suspiciously. She was not, I thought, as naturally superstitious as the Boxer peasantry, but I believed that a person at the end of her rope would grasp at a myth when nothing else was available. Still, she surprised me yet again.

"Do the cannons not already shoot high," she said, "and have some of my greatest generals not kept themselves absent from the field? If I were truly determined to take the foreign Enclave, do you really believe there would be a single soul alive there still?"

Before I could answer, though, or even absorb the import of this statement, there was a shout from without.

A eunuch, his state of panic overcoming his propriety and propelling him into the chamber unannounced, brought us the reason. A fire started in a shop that offered foreign goods (a blaze, I thought, almost surely sparked by Huo) had spread beyond control, igniting the 30-meter tall Qianmen Gate, a portal only opened for the Emperor during seasonal prayers. It was a tsunami of an omen, fit to wash away my hurried attempt at myth-making.

The Empress addressed the eunuch, eyes flashing with a new determination, or perhaps it was merely desperation.

"Bring guards and see that this self-professed Red Lantern enjoys the hospitality of one of our prison cells. Perhaps the peace and quiet will enable her to gather her thoughts and speak sense, or will at the least reveal to me whose creature she is."

I could certainly have resisted and won my freedom, but only at the cost of my ruse and my mission. So I allowed myself to be led off, determined to maintain my facade in the face of anything short of the executioner's axe. It was only when the stone door swung shut upon my prison that I remembered that my eye-drops were in the bedroll that had been unceremoniously stripped from me on the way to my incarceration.

At least I had recently fed, and since the sun nowhere intruded into my cell, I would be able to rest and not risk the pain and slow depletion caused by excessive exposure to daylight.

Chapter Ten

It is said that time passes slowly for the imprisoned, but that is largely a mortal conceit. Spared the tedious timekeeping of sun and moon, and, if I husbanded my energy, in no immediate need to procure nourishment, I experienced a rare freedom. After locating a scraped-away depression that more or less accommodated my hip, and scooping together a small mound of detritus to serve as pillow, I was able to leave my body to this relative comfort and retreat into a low-level consciousness, as a great Machine will idle easily when not under load.

I was of course interrupted once a day by the delivery of my poor inmate's portion of food and water. This proved a boon, as I soon persuaded a small army of rodents to eliminate the foodstuffs and give the impression that I ate. Of course by conditioning these creatures to materialize at the ring of bowl upon stone, I also assured myself of an emergency source of sustenance should my incarceration last that long. Leftover water, mixed with whatever droppings were produced by my dinner guests, provided proof of my intestinal regularity unpleasant enough to discourage close study.

I learned little of the outside during my stay. The walls were proof against any noise, and my daily human visitors were silent. The faint fragrance of smoke on their clothes, however, told me that parts of the city still burned, and that the siege of the foreigner's compound had thus likely not yet reached a bloody and successful conclusion. I wondered if Cixi were indeed holding back her hand, and if her own strategies were truly as Machiavellian as Lady Ellen's, or my own.

What I did not know, my cell being absent any mirror and even the ceramic bowl that carried my daily delivery proven incapable of reflection (and such are as visible to the Kin as to anyone, regardless of the presumptions of Fiction), was how my irises might be reacting to their time without my eye drops. I speculated that the darkness in my confinement might have slowed their return to normal, but had no way of verifying this theory. I could only determine to keep my eyes downcast when freed, at least until I could somehow recover my bedroll and reapply the dye, or at least verify the latter necessity.

That occasion came sooner than I might have expected, and thus most of my four-legged companions were spared the need to pay the ultimate price for the thin rice gruel they'd so been enjoying. In fact, I cannot have been too many days in solitude when the sounds of a disturbance from without shook me from my ruminative reverie. I rose to my feet, brushing my costume clean of the grit of the floor and, eyes downcast and partially hidden by the disarray of my hair, I prepared for whatever the fates might bring me.

I speculated that the Dowager Empress had perhaps had second thoughts, or even merely was curious to see if my days in seclusion had loosened my tongue, or had simply decided to do away with me once and for all in a fit of anger. I also considered that perhaps Huo was behind the ruckus without, having some need for me to further her own schemes, or simply happy to take the opportunity to demonstrate yet again that even Cixi was subject to her whims and wishes.

When the door was opened by a still stubborn if thoroughly cowed eunuch, I saw that my speculation had not ventured far enough afield. For waiting there to escort me from dungeon and palace alike was neither Empress nor creature, but none other than Li-hua, the sense of triumph on her pretty features unable to quite mask the nervousness that her efforts on my behalf had engendered.

"You are remarkable," she said. "Only a miracle worker of the first order could manage to be imprisoned by the Qing at a time when the Empire is our champion and ally. Then again, were your case not so unusual I might not have even heard of your incarceration. Now come with me before I regret the chances I've taken to reach you here."

"But the Empress..." I began, in an attempt to make clear to my friend the level of risk she had assumed.

"The Dowager has forgotten you, Liu, and if I were wise I would have done the same. Although she has an Empire to lose and I have only my head. Now come, before some errant Mandarin decides to curry favor with the regime by hindering your escape."

Fortunately the sight of two Red Lanterns in the Forbidden City was not the outrage it would have recently been (with a number of the residents now affecting red clothing), and we were able to hurry through the corridors without attracting anything more than curiosity. Once in the Imperial City itself, we did not draw even such attention. Every second individual seemed to be a Boxer or Red Lantern or interested in appearing to be such. Li-hua led me through the crowds and into a neat courtyard surrounding a dwelling that seemed remarkably free from damage giving the chaos that surrounded it. I dared mention as much and she answered with a knowing laugh.

"It belongs to a Prince," she said. "He was persuaded to present it to the Lanterns for our use for the duration of the troubles. Of course, if he had not done do we would have simply taken it." At the heart of the dwelling, behind a sturdy mahogany door, we came upon what was apparently the princely bedroom, with a large brick kang luxuriously appointed with silks and pillows. Li-hua settled me here, and addressed me with lingering sternness, though she was unable to prevent herself from fiddling with the ruin of my hair, forcing me to keep my head down and look all the more contrite as she groomed me.

"You will wish to wash, certainly, Sister-disciple," she said," but first I must examine your wound."

I rolled onto my stomach, my once-wounded side toward her. Li-hua pulled my shirt up, and greeted the sight of my unmarked skin with a sharp intake of breath.

"There is nothing," she said, breathless, her fingers tracing the area where I'd been stabbed.

I raised my bottom, as a cat will lift itself to encourage further petting.

"There is magic in your touch," I whispered. "I knew it."

She gasped again, softer this time, and her fingers lingered, slipping down my side and toward my stomach beneath. I lifted my body again, allowing access, but Li-hua pulled her hand away as if stung.

"I will bring you water," she said, hurriedly. "And then we must rest, it grows dark.

She did so, the bowl was warm and a cloth floated atop it. My companion tip-toed out and I washed myself hurriedly, slipping out of the snug red trousers and, before calling her back, tugging the hem of my short-sleeved top down over my hips.

The room was quite dark when she returned, though I could see her clearly. She had removed her soft shoes and, as I had, slipped out of her trousers. She had washed as well; I could still smell the warm water on her. I wriggled aside to make room as she arranged herself next to me on the kang.

Li-hua touched my cheek, just enough to guide herself, and dared a chaste peck of a kiss on my mouth before curling with her back toward me.

"Goodnight, Liu," she whispered, "perhaps we can steal a few hours of rest before I have to rescue you again." I laughed in reply, and settled myself next to her, back to back.

It soon became clear that my bed-mate was unquiet. She would be still for a moment, and then squirm as if to seek a more pleasing position. I allowed this to continue for some time, and eventually felt her round backside brush against mine.

I moved just enough to press more firmly against her, and felt her withdraw and then tentatively return, her restlessness growing more obvious.

"You cannot sleep, Li-hua?" I breathed into a handful of silk clutched in the hand beneath my chin.

She was quiet for a moment, and then whispered a reply.

"The air is warm and the bricks are cold," she said. "It is difficult to find comfort."

I stretched and turned, cupping my body against her from behind. I counted on her distress to hide the chill of my contact, and it seemed to do so, though I was delightfully aware of the heat of her skin beneath the short shirt.

"Perhaps if we were closer?" I let my breath play upon the back of her neck, breathing in the perfume with which she had dressed her black hair.

"Perhaps..." she whispered, and I slipped my upper arm around her, pulling her near.

"What are you doing, Liu?" There was no protest in her voice, and she pushed back against me despite herself

"Shsssh," I cooed, "only getting more comfortable." My mouth was close now, close enough for her to feel my lips move against her skin.

She half turned, twisting her head to face me in the dark, her mouth half opened to speak again, and I kissed her, once, twice. She started to protest, but there was no heart in it. I kissed her more deeply, demanding, and she let me turn her fully to face me and slid her own arm around my waist. As she did I slipped a knee between her naked legs and felt them part as she rode up upon the smooth intrusion of my thigh.

Once admitted to, her passion could not be contained, and I soon had her red shirt off and added to the tangle of silks around us. She cried out as my fingers first captured her breasts, pinching and stroking, and finally entered her below. Her voice stifled by my mouth; she whimpered again and again, soft, imploring, until her back arched and her muscles clenched and thrummed, leaving her limp and breathless.

Her eyes were wide in the dark; though she could see little of me as I dressed her with many soft kisses, and pulled her close against me again.

"What did you do?" She asked, pleasure-addled and shocked at where her body had taken her.

"That is just one rescue repaid," I whispered, holding her tightly as she shivered toward sleep. Li-hua had done nothing to reciprocate my attentions, but I believed that would be an adventure for another time, as would another form of pleasure I might share with her. For the moment, I resolved to be patient, and was admittedly quite pleased with myself all the same.

I did not sleep that night, and limited my movement so as not to disturb my companion's rest. I did, however, manage to survey the contents of the room we shared, and was pleased to see that Li-hua had somehow managed to free my bedroll as well as me, and had stashed it in a corner of the chamber, apparently without exploring its contents.

I was contemplating how I might best use my current situation to further my objectives (and I confess musing about how to expand my relationship with my bedmate) when movement beside me indicated that the sleeper was waking. The sun had clearly risen, cutting thin strips of light between the slatted bamboo that covered the small window, and I sat up to lean over and welcome her with a smile.

Li-hua was as yet half asleep, squinting against the morning, but her thoughts were clearly still lingering on the events of the prior evening. She made bold to reach for my shoulders and pull me into a good-morning kiss, which I happily granted, noting that she had not forgotten the lessons I'd taught her in the darkness. When we broke the kiss, however, she looked me full in the face, about to renew our dalliance, only to stop and stare, mouth open in shock.

"Your eyes!" She managed only those two words before breaking away from me and scrambling across the floor on hands and knees. I flirted briefly with the notion of fabricating some sort of explanation, but the poor girl was obviously terrified, and all of the demons of her superstitions were arisen and arrayed against me.

I had barely a moment before she recovered enough to call for aid, and so leapt from the kang myself, only half clothed. Grabbing up my roll from where I'd previously marked it, I bolted from the privacy of that commandeered room and into the ongoing chaos outside, her screams behind me adding impetus to my flight.

My options were suddenly very limited. Were I to stay in red, even after availing myself of my eye drops, I would surely run afoul of Li-hua again, as she (thanks in no little part to the role I'd played in her miraculous healing) was, if not a person of authority, still held in high regard among the Boxers and Lanterns. It would also not do to remind the Qing of my existence, particularly when the Empress had last seen me shut away in a cell.

Though Li-hua's cries were concentrating a cluster of attention behind, none of this had yet focused upon me, and I was able to slip unseen into a hovel consisting of two standing walls and the partially collapsed roof of a burned building. The quarters there were close, and stank of smoke, but offered space enough for me to strip out of my Lantern shirt and don the set of blue clothing that had been stuffed into my pack. I discarded my spare suit of peasant dress, seeing no need for the opulence of a change of clothes, but was unable to force myself to abandon my Lantern blouse, believing that it might yet prove useful. I also managed to insert my eye drops, though I spilled some of the liquid on my cheeks as a result of working blindly. This was little worry, as it would be to my benefit if they could pass for dirty tears.

With no other option available to me, I refastened my bedroll, slung it over my shoulder and when the constantly shifting patterns of rebels and their Imperial allies opened a brief path, broke from my shelter and sprinted toward the barricaded Legations.

Immediately a hue and cry went up. I would surely have drawn suspicion enough in my peasant dress, which marked me as not affiliated with the uprising, but my flight toward the hated foreign devils identified me clearly as an enemy. I was determined, too, to move at a speed that did not show me to be other than mortal, stinging still as I was from the carelessness that had allowed Li-hua to see my blue eyes.

So the Boxers were uncomfortably close, and I was keenly aware that, should I be forced to fight my way clear, a single sweep of sword or axe could end Paulette Monot's story before it had rightly begun. I jinked and dodged, like a fox before hounds, aware of the occasional boom of black-powder gun shots behind me and the hiss and whine of bullets flying uncomfortably close.

Suddenly, however, there was rifle fire in front of me as well, and a barricade was swung wide to reveal a small force of Westerners racing toward me, shooting rapidly as they ran. I allowed myself to stumble into the arms of one of these and, his companions lingering behind to make things hot for the pursuing Boxers, was half-carried through the rough defenses and into the relative safety of the Legation Quarter.

CHAPTER ELEVEN

I collapsed on the ground there, my sobs little more than half artifice, only to be helped to my feet by the tallest of my saviors, a fair-haired man with a lean, intelligent face who surprised me by addressing me (with no little suspicion in his tones) in halting, heavily accented, Manchu.

"Are you Christian, girl?" he demanded; and none too gently, I thought, considering the ordeal I'd clearly been through.

"Yes, yes," I stammered back, slipping between the language he spoke and pidgin English. "Hail Mary, Our Father...oh God my family, they have killed them all."

"How you live so long," he continued, now in broken English to match my own, and still clearly not mollified.

I was glad for the evidence offered by the smoke reek on my clothes.

"I hide in burned places," I said, "eat dead rats and dogs. But they find me. I not know where I run, but go as long as my legs go."

As I spoke I took advantage of the opportunity to more closely examine my inquisitor. He looked to be in his late thirties, close to six feet tall and athletic, with fair hair and blue eyes almost piercing enough to match my own true color. There was an air of impatient intelligence about him, as if he saw things that others did not, and rued the inability of the world to keep pace with his thoughts.

These were all qualities, of course, that I found most attractive in a man (and, in truth, perhaps my recent adventure with Li-hua had excited my libido). I caught myself wondering if my disguise would incite racist repulsion or exotic attraction. Since I had no immediate plans beyond survival in my precarious setting, I resolved to explore the matter as possibilities arose.

I came out of this reverie to realize that my rescuers were discussing what would become of me. The consensus seemed to be that I should be put in the Fu, a nobleman's residence that had been appropriated for the use of the Chinese Christians, a separation decreed by lingering class distinctions and, I think, by the xenophobia which, in the wake of the Boxer's atrocities, caused all Westerners to look upon all Cantonese with some trepidation. (I later learned that this acquisition had been engineered by the rescuer who had drawn my interest, in much the same way that Li-hua had "negotiated" the use of the dwelling in which she stayed.) Further comments led me to understand that the Fu was already overcrowded, and its residents desperately short of food.

Though such conditions would have served my needs nicely, I feared that once lost among the starving hordes I would be forgotten, and condemned to what would certainly be a dreary existence for the immediate future. Thus I decided to weight the die in my favor and spoke again, slowly as if searching for the correct words, but evidencing a greater fluency, however accented it might be. I did this both because it would provide me access to information that might benefit my Lady, and for more lascivious reasons of my own.

"Please," I said, "I speak English and Machu. Maybe I can be of help?"

The tall man turned away from his companions to face me.

"Can you read?" he said.

"Yes, a little English, a little Manchu," I replied. The latter was a fabrication, however. Lady Ellen had not considered reading Chinese to be important to my masquerade, since such abilities were supposedly rare among those in the Middle Kingdom's countryside. If it were necessary to bluff to achieve my aims, however, then charade I would, and count on my Kindred language skills to come through in the end.

"What is your name?" he asked.

"Jinyu Liu," I replied, averting my eyes politely.

"I am George Morrison, Miss Jinyu," he replied, using my surname correctly. "If you are as clever as you say, I might have work for you. If not, well, I trust I'll discover that soon enough. You may come with me."

I overheard some whispering as he led me away, speculating on my figure beneath the shapeless peasant clothes and the sort of work that George Morrison might require of me, but I gave no sign that I could hear such speculation and followed him politely.

His dwelling was of modest size but well maintained, with concrete-latticed windows and sliding papered doors. It showed little sign of the struggle beyond the compound, save for a few bullet-marks on the walls and a circular stain on the patio, surrounded by a few specks of dark earth, where a flower pot had perhaps been hit by a fleeing foot or random missile and the detritus quickly but inexpertly swept away.

Inside I was shown a kitchen, what I assumed was the master bedroom (with a kang, desk, chair, and typewriter, where I guessed the master of the house was wont to pursue his daily labors), a large guest room that I learned I was to share with the rest of his servants, and a simple shower and bathroom. The household staff consisted of a cook and several others (the numbers seemed to fluctuate, as if some were absent carrying messages and such even in these uncertain times). There seemed little enough to do in the small dwelling for such a number, but I presumed Morrison had once needed more and was loathe to abandon his loyal staffers to the poor comforts of the Fu.

My new housemates greeted me with understandable suspicion, since to their eyes I was little more than another mouth to feed with what I was sure was a finite stockpile of rations. I took the edge off of this concern, at least temporarily, by pleading exhaustion as a result of my recent ordeal and begging them to share my first meal among themselves. This consisted of a rather poor quality rice that had apparently been cooked in the broth left over from some sort of vegetable destined for the master's table, and spiced with a bit of nondescript grey meat. However unappealing it appeared to me, however, I noted that it disappeared quite rapidly.

There were, I learned, many more Chinese kept in the Fu's unofficial quarantine than there were representatives of the European nations and Japan in the legation quarter. These "coolies" (for so there were called, even by the best of the foreigners) were responsible for building and maintaining most of the fortifications protecting the entire compound, and were worked mercilessly whether in rain, or heat, or beneath a hail-fall of bullets. I never heard a concrete estimation of their numbers; it was only clear that more were arriving daily as surviving missionaries delivered the bedraggled remnants of their flocks into shelter, and rescue groups, such as the Morrison-led party that had brought me in, dared the wrath of the Boxers to retrieve others.

The food provided these unfortunates was, from what I was able to overhear, for the most part wholesome but lacking in quantity. Of course, we were all in a state of siege, and rations would likely be drawn tighter before they were loosened. I felt quite sure the greater burden of this conservation would be borne by those in the Fu.

I slept through the remainder of that day, and appeared to do so during the night as well, though my senses were active in the dark hours and I was eager for whatever information they might purloin from my quiet surroundings. None of these discoveries were noteworthy, at least initially. The night was filled with hints as to the nocturnal habits of my housemates, the schedules of the enclave's watch, and the predilection for evening military activity on the part of the unsavory elements in various portions of the city. But it is with such details that a map is filled, and the less particular one's map, the greater the potential for a misstep.

A general bustle in the rooms just prior to sunrise announced the beginning of a new day. It seemed that Morrison was an early riser, particularly during hot spells when he preferred to tackle his chores before the sun became oppressive and rest during the afternoon (a habit which suited me nicely). Upon rising, I made myself as presentable as possible using the few tools at my command and prepared for the anticipated summoning.

When it came, it was not in the form of the personal visit to my shared quarters that I'd expected, but in that of the distant tinkling of a small bell. My roommates noticed my ignorance of the meaning of this sound, and with many an urgent whisper and shooing propelled me to Morrison's room, where I found him already seated at his desk.

"Miss Jinyu," he said by way of welcome. "I trust you rested and have recovered from your ordeal?"

I nodded in reply, and he continued.

"Grand. We shall start with some simple matters. I have here a group of handbills that my agents have liberated from walls within the city. If you would be so kind, could you tell me the import of each? There is no need for exact translation, a summary will suit my purposes as well."

Though I could of course understand him perfectly, I took a moment to seem to puzzle over his formal diction before nodding again, at which he slid a small stack of posters across the desk toward me and waited, pen poised in his hand.

These were public notices, and so for the most part were expressed in the simplest language, particularly those generated by the Boxers and their allies. (I assumed the intent of these was that they would be deciphered by the few who could read, and their meaning then conveyed to the illiterate.) The first that fell to hand was one of the latter, and its message had been etched into my mind by repetition.

"This one calls upon the people to support the Qing and kill all the foreigners," I said.

Rather than simply accept the information, my employer immediately turned upon me with a question that cut to the heart of the matter.

"And when," he said, "did the rebels add support for the Regime to their calls for murder and mayhem?"

I had of course not been privy to the Imperial correspondence, but had heard and seen much in my time on the road and (however briefly) in Court, and thus was able to provide an answer that I thought accurate.

"I believe the words were first added some days ago in Tientsin," I said. "Though I suspect this might have been done before the Dowager officially threw her support to the Boxers."

He leaned his elbows on the desk, cupped his chin in his hands and regarded me.

"And why, do you think, did the usually wise Cixi make sure an egregious error?"

I immediately saw that I was being tested, and that, should I pass, my role would expand from mere translator to advisor. This had the potential to lead to further benefits, and thus I answered carefully, remembering the Empress's own words.

"I think she believed she had no choice," I said. "I think she feared an invasion, and saw her navy in ruins and her army helpless. I think she saw the people of China as her final hope."

"An astute answer, Miss Jinyu," he replied after some thought. "I believe I made a wise decision to keep you here and not allow you to be sent to the Fu."

I had learned of my host's occupation from the gossip in my quarters, so replied politely.

"I hope to further justify that belief, Journalist Morrison," I said.

He laughed in recognition of my initiative. "You may address me as George, which is my given name, Miss Jinyu," he replied. "Might I ask the same allowance?"

I cast my eyes down again and nodded modestly.

"I am called Liu, if it pleases you," I said.

He clapped his hands in satisfaction, briefly startling me.

"Capital!" He said. "Though I imagine it would be your name whether it pleased me or no! And now perhaps we can proceed on a less formal basis."

I experimented at allowing a blush, and did feel the rush of it in my cheeks, though I did not know how clearly it manifested itself under my dyed skin. George smiled in reply, so even if he saw nothing of the coloration he read my expression well enough.

We worked through various other handbills, including Cixi's original proclamation outlawing the Boxers, which she had issued before her change of heart. I was able to parse out the sense of these fairly easily, and as the morning progressed George graduated me to more complex documents, some of which seemed to have been issued by the Empire and others which appeared to be purloined communications between factions of the Chinese army.

These I was less adroit at deciphering, but was able to translate a word here and there and, with the help of information I had gleaned in my travels and a bit of educated guesswork, proved capable of pleasing my benefactor for the most part. When we had finished the first rank of the documents, he leaned back in his chair and regarded me before speaking again.

"Tell me, Liu, what do you personally think will become of China in the wake of the recent disorders?

It seemed that I was being tested again, and knowing nothing of George's views I cast back to my discussions with Lady Ellen before replying.

"The question, I think," I said, picking my way carefully, "will be whether the country is carved up among the Powers or survives as a nation that will be developed and modernized through the more peaceful avenues of commerce. I fear that the answer might hinge upon the fate of these Legations." I perhaps did not speak quite so clearly as I transcribe it here, but even with the disguise of accent the sophistication of my answer triggered a rise of his eyebrows.

"There is perhaps more to you than you make out, Liu." He said.

I took the opportunity to meet eyes with him briefly and favor him with a quick smile.

"Such could be said of all women, or at least should, George." I answered.

He laughed. "Would that it were true, Liu, but I find most of your gender are far less complex than they make themselves out to be."

"Onions without layers?" I said, cutting my eyes away shyly.

"Perhaps I can offer a better metaphor?" He countered. "For an onion is nothing *but* layers, with no secret to be revealed, where the artichoke is peeled to expose the sweetness of its heart."

I blushed again. Whether he could see it or no it seemed both prudent and good practice (it is a skill that rewards such repetition), after which I pointedly busied myself with the papers remaining on his desk.

I believe he feared that he had been too bold; and though I'd carefully led him toward those words, I allowed him his misconception. Our unstated flirtation had the added effect of quite distracting him from my rapidly growing facility with English. In this manner we were all of a sudden more closely joined. It is, after all, with such small steps that all great dances begin.

Chapter Twelve

My first day of working for George Morrison established a pattern. We would begin very early with some relatively simple translations (which I found myself rapidly becoming more capable of deciphering), and gradually work through more complicated documents, with my efforts at these occasionally interrupted as he asked my opinion of some matter or another. After the first day, however, he was the soul of decorum and made not the slightest effort to flirt with me. Something certainly had to be done.

It was a delicate situation, even for one of my appetites and talents. Given the social demographics of our relationship, I feared that any boldness on my part would further compromise my disguise and perhaps even drive my would-be paramour away. As the days passed (each punctuated regularly with the rattle of gunshot and the percussion of cannon shell; I found myself quite ignoring it after a while) I considered my options and awaited an opportunity.

Worse yet, I had only the one outfit, the blue peasant clothes I had brought with me from London (as well as the telltale short-sleeved red shirt rolled tightly up in my bag). So I simply bathed as often as possible (to the point that I think my fellow "converts" looked upon me as if I were deranged), and took every opportunity to dress my hair in flowers scavenged from the planters still tended within the Legation grounds, particularly those which had a lingering scent.

I could of course have, when the door was shut upon us, subjected George to the now considerable Entrancement of my eyes, which as I had proven to myself while on the road had not been diluted by the dye I used. I rejected this option out of hand, however. After all, a girl must have her pride.

As it turned out, my apparently excessive attention to cleanliness provided the first opportunity to move the dance forward. Over the course of a few days, I discovered that my roommates could occasionally be relied upon to quit our shared quarters early, perhaps when the anticipated household duties were predicted to be especially time consuming, and thus leave me with some moments of privacy there that were not so reliably to be found in the shared bath quarters. On one such occasion I hurried to the kitchen to beg a bowl of hot water and returned to wash in solitude. I pulled the paper-screened door to and, stripping off the garments that covered the upper part of my body, kneeled on the floor and set to sponging myself clean with a scrap of cloth.

I perhaps luxuriated too long in this bathing, and was still in the process when I heard the bright little sound of the bell announcing the beginning of the day's labors. Sensing an opportunity, I continued as I was, closing my eyes as I scrubbed my face and then moving down to wash my breasts and belly. While my lids were still closed, I heard the rattle of the door being slid open and turned, blinking the water away, to see my employer framed in the doorway.

His eyes were on my bosom (he was a man after all!), still wet and glistening. I covered myself with my hands, perhaps being a bit slow in doing so, and turned to favor him with a view of the elegant line of my back.

"Excuse me Liu," he said. "I did not know."

Standing, with my back still to him, I struggled into my top, perhaps gracing him with another glimpse of the firm sway of a breast before he turned away in confusion.

"It is I who should be sorry, George. I must have had water in my ears when the bell rang!" I said, all a-fluster. I hastily returned the cloth to its bowl and stood, tugging my shirt over the wet body beneath, the latter betraying itself in cunning outline where the damp skin clung to the cotton.

It was his turn to blush, and he did so quite dramatically before turning and walking to his room. I followed politely, knowing that he would not soon forget the scene that he had walked in upon. George seated himself when we were both in his quarters, and began to speak again, obviously still in some distress.

"I must apologize again," he said. "I was not aware that you used the servants' quarters for bathing."

"They had all left," I explained, apparently distraught myself, "I only hoped for a bit of privacy, which is hard to come by elsewhere."

"If you wish seclusion," he said, "I can offer you the use of this room in the future."

"With you here?" I managed to sound quite scandalized.

He blushed mightily again.

"No, but of course not. You have only to let me know when you require it and I will find reason to be absent."

It would have been easy to make some flirtatious comment about needing someone to wash my back, but the task at hand called for more delicacy than that, so I averted my eyes again and spoke apologetically.

"That is kind of you," I said. "It is difficult for a woman to feel pretty in times like these. I find my spirits are buoyed when I look after my appearance as much as is possible."

George rose to the bait gallantly, as I'd hoped he would.

"Surely you know that you are very beautiful, Liu." He said.

I met his eyes then, though made no effort to Enchant but only to hold his gaze when he did not look away. We maintained this contact for long moments, before I spoke in a small, breathless voice.

"If you think so, then I am a very happy girl," I said.

It was most gratifying to watch this exceptional man struggle with himself. I knew he had been alone for a long while, his only company the embassy staff whom he looked down upon and the chilly companionship of correspondence. In comparison to that, he and I had shared a form of intimacy, however proscribed, and this was now augmented and complicated by the images of my nakedness that he must have been unable to delete from his memory.

It was a close thing, and I let it be his decision. If I had taken a step toward him I knew he would have opened his arms. If he had so much as reached toward me I would have stepped. He mastered himself, however, and so we resumed the daily schedule as if nothing had happened. I knew, however, that our *pas de deux* had begun, and that it was neither he nor Jinyu Liu, but Paulette Monot who was calling the steps.

Such dances take time, though, and the workday proceeded apace until, while I was in the throes of translating a rather difficult court document, obtained I knew not how, George stopped me by placing a finger upon the page.

"I need to know of Tientsin, Liu," he said. "We must know if and when relief will come if we are to plan well enough to survive this siege."

I had no surfeit of information on which to base an answer, and mentally inventoried that data rapidly; Seymour's isolation and dilemma, my own experiences outside of the walls of the harried Western quarters in that city, and Huo's sarcastic prophecies. I took all of these into account before replying, but found myself relying most heavily on the musings of the latter creature, though I knew she was devious and mercurial and not entirely to be trusted.

"Relief will come, I believe," I said, "but not as quickly as the optimists among the Delegations would hope. The siege in Tientsin will ultimately fail merely because it has moved too slowly. The rains are returning, and the Boxers will go back to their lands. Seymour will turn from Pekin and trace his steps back there, and Western troops from the sea must be arriving soon. Only when the Powers have broken the attack and taken that city in its entirely will they be emboldened enough to turn their thoughts and their armies toward Pekin. This is what I believe, though I do not claim any gift of prophecy."

Morrison digested this information in silence before speaking.

"Soothsayer or no, Liu, I think you have more nearly the right of it than the self-proclaimed Merlins in our leadership here and in the Foreign Office. Seymour's force would have been here by now had it not encountered unexpected and calamitous delays, and if that is the case our compatriots in Tientsin might well find themselves in a situation analogous to our own. Do you think," he continued, a fingertip rubbing his chin, "that a messenger could reach that town to tell them of our situation and return with news?"

It had not been long, of course, since I had walked the road between the two cities, and so I answered with a bit more confidence.

"There are armies other than Seymour's along the route," I said, "and fortifications growing. The crops are head-high or greater for much of the way, however, and I believe that an individual capable of withstanding the heat and insects could use them as cover, journeying by night, and arrive successfully. Once in Tientsin, though, he would needs find a way into the barricaded areas without being beheaded by the attackers or summarily shot by the defenders."

"I believe I have just the man for the job," Morrison announced, snapping his fingers. "A red scarf for his head should provide some protection from the Boxers and Imperials, and a few words in English would perhaps stay the guns of the West and allow him to deliver his message safely. I'll need you to write out two missives for me, one in English and the other in Manchu, can you do that?"

His question was a matter of form only; George by then knew quite well that I could now do what he asked and would do so without question. So rather than give a more fulsome reply I merely nodded and, taking up a pen and ink bottle from the desk, selected two sheets of paper and prepared for the work.

"In English," Morrison dictated, "simply say that we are desperate and have finite supplies of food and ammunition, and very much require a realistic estimate as to when relief might be expected to arrive so as to order to husband our resources appropriately.

"The other document, in Manchu, should proclaim that the carrier is acting in the service of the Dowager Empress and that all loyal Chinese are urged to give him any aid possible Make it appear as official as you can." He paused, nodding to himself. "Put both in whatever words you choose. I'll be back momentarily with our messenger boy."

I had not anticipated that George meant "boy" so literally. Before I had finished the characters in the second document (which were far more time consuming to pen than are the letters of our dear old Mother Tongue, while creating an approximation of the seals used by the Dowager required my steadiest hand and greatest patience), he returned to the room leading a lad whom I had seen once before begging scraps from the kitchen. As I came to understand, the apparent urchin had been for some time in Morrison's employ, was well fed as a result, and only pestered our cook as a way of "keeping his hand in," as George explained it to me, using the vernacular comfortably.

This guttersnipe's given name was Jie. It is difficult to determine age in this society where malnutrition is a playmate and starvation the wicked uncle always threatening to visit, but he could not have been older than fourteen. I presented the documents to Morrison. He studied them briefly (though he could not read a single character of Manchu, but such is the vanity of even the better sort of man) before presenting them to his messenger.

"This one," he waved the English message and spoke in that tongue, "fold tightly and secrete upon yourself, and be prepared to eat it if necessary, for I fear that having it discovered upon your person would be the equivalent of a death warrant. Once you reach the foreigners in Tientsin deliver it to any one of the concession leaders. I'd of course prefer it go to the British man in charge, though I do not know who that might be.

"This," and here he presented Jie with the forged Chinese document, "subject to water and dust staining as soon as you safely can; and fold and refold it until the creases are weak. The more difficult it is to read in its entirely the better it will serve you if needed."

In response the youth carefully folded the former document and made it vanish within the roll of his sash. The latter he spat upon, folded roughly, and pushed into his underclothes. I had no doubt that after a few miles in such an unfortunate hiding place the missive would be reduced to a state that only the most officious of Imperial or Boxer dogsbodies would venture to examine it closely.

These things accomplished, George also presented the boy with a sack containing, I assumed, rice and coin and other necessities for the road, and bid him safe journey. Not a word was spoken by the unlikely messenger before he departed on his mission, and I wondered if he were indeed mute and would thus be forced to let my documents speak for him in the face of whatever contingencies he might meet along the road.

I turned to my employer seeking an explanation.

"Surely you told him to keep to the fields and avoid the road?" I asked. "Seymour has stirred up a hornet's nest out there, I'm quite certain of this."

"Yes, Liu, I've given Jie all the information he requires. He is a stickler for instruction, but cannot hold too many in his poor head at one time. Hence I did not feel it prudent to have a beautiful woman speak to him as well as me, and thus complicate matters unnecessarily.

The compliment was nicely hidden, so well that I decided to pretend it was undetected and see where the conversation might thus lead.

"Thank you," I said, "I am concerned that he will undertake this mission with only my poor Manchu script for protection."

"You discredit yourself, pretty Liu," Morrison replied. "I'm confident that Jie's wits and your forgery will be armor enough for any event that might befall him."

Thus Morrison piled flattery upon compliment, to a point where I would have been churlish to ignore both.

I raised my eyes to his, without Enchantment I assure you, though in truth they might have sparkled just a touch more than would be natural.

"That is thrice you have mentioned my appearance, George, do you seek by such a spell to draw me to you?"

It is possible he was unaware of the impact of his words, as a man speaking the truth might be blind to the pain or pleasure his statements inspire. He stared at me for a moment, with a delightful look of almost childlike wonder on his handsome face, and then wordlessly turned and in two long strides had closed the paper screen that joined his quarters to the rest of the house. For my part I played the innocent wanton; I merely stood watching him with my dark eyes wide, my lips wet and just parted, and stroking the end of my long fall of black hair in one hand.

There had been rumors aplenty about Morrison, as there will be concerning any attractive single man in a community of expatriates. He had been linked with any number of hopeful embassy wives, rumored to employ courtesans and ravage eligible Chinese girls by the score, connected in scandalous whispers to a number of attractive young men, and was even reputed to have been one of Cixi's lovers. Within seconds of finding myself in his arms I knew that these one and all were untrue.

He lifted me onto the desk, already kissing me as if he would die without the touch of my mouth. I protested weakly, in an effort to seem appropriately coy and in so doing to inflame his ardor. This my whimpers did, and I knew that his passion was that of a man whose physical urges had been long suppressed.

It was not an occasion to display my versatility. George struggled with my simple clothing, and only managed to expose my breasts with some surreptitious help from yours truly. He was so overcome by their revelation that I feared he would spend himself while adoring them with his lips and tongue. He somehow got me out of my trousers, however, and seemed not to notice the practiced cleverness of my hands as I freed him from the essential parts of his far more complicated wardrobe (for he, like most men in the Enclave, bedecked himself in full suit and vest despite, of perhaps because of, the crisis boiling just behind the barricades).

My lover had a beautiful body, perhaps gone slightly soft with desk work but still clearly the form of a man of action. I explored it with my hands and mouth, and when his cock was free guided it with one slim hand to where I wanted it, confident that his passion would not allow him to question the cool slickness of my depths.

He did not, but plunged desperately, my knees high and heels crossed over his back. So fierce was his desire that it was only moments before I felt the searing heat of his explosion deep inside me, and continued to rock against his penetration as he grew smaller and softer.

Panting, he stood then, confused and guilty, trying with clumsy hands to cover my nakedness with the clothing that he had not completely removed.

"I'm sorry dear Liu," he stammered, "I could not help myself."

Pushing myself up with my arms, I kissed his stomach, noting with satisfaction that this brought new tremors to his now flaccid cock.

"No George, no apology is required," I whispered, "I wanted it as well, I want it still. I would be your lover if you will have me."

He held my head to his stomach, and I ventured to slide lower beneath his hands, kissing the base of his cock until it began to rise again in reply to the attentions of my mouth. He growled low in the back of his throat.

"No, Liu, no, there is no need for that."

But by then I had run my tongue around the tip and he was fully erect. With my dark eyes on his, making sure he saw my hunger in then, I slipped my mouth over him and took him in as deeply as I dared, choking slightly in my eagerness.

His hands were on my head, but I raised it slowly nonetheless until he was quite free of my lips again, and fully erect. I kissed the tip almost chastely, and smiled up at him.

"There was need before, it seems, but none now." With this I leaned back on the table, my knees wide.

With a small, helpless cry he entered me again. Our coupling was slower this time, and I controlled the pace with the lifting of my hips against him, whimpering his name with each penetration, as I knew the response of the partner is perhaps the most erotic of all components of lovemaking. He lasted longer than before, but his climax was no less explosive, and seemed to shake him from his shoulders to his knees.

Chapter Thirteen

It took me only moments to pull on my blue clothing, and just a bit longer to help button George into his suit and vest. He was nervous as I did the latter, and continued to try to assist me, but I brushed his hands aside and soon had him looking every inch the distinguished correspondent again.

"There," I said, standing in front of him now and smoothing his jacket. "My pretty man is all back together with his dignity intact!"

"And his life forever changed!" said George, taking my hands in his. "You will of course stay here with me now."

"I will do no such thing," I said, gripping his hands tightly in mine. "To live with me openly and unwed would tarnish your reputation forever; and we are nowhere near to marrying, darling, as if that would be any less of a scandal. You shall have me when your wishes and mine coincide. I promise you will find that to be every bit as often as you could dream it to be."

"You are," he began, then released me to throw his hands in the air in exasperation, "you are quite unlike any woman I have ever known."

"I should hope so!" I preened prettily for his amusement. "Better to not be in the game at all than to be second!"

Such behavior was reckless, and the sophistication of my language more so, to be sure, but my dear George's mind was far too overcome with dealing with recent events to make the leap to questioning anything about me; though that was soon to change.

I had, however, put the onus for initiating further escapades firmly upon him. This left me unable to seek my satisfaction as often as I'd like, perhaps, but I felt sure that, having tasted the forbidden fruit, my George would not long stay away from its tree.

Sadly enough, he did have the little matter of the siege to distract him. The bombardments remained a daily occurrence, as did the long-distance shooting of the Imperial troops (and perhaps I was fooling myself, but it did seem that their shots were uniformly high), and the occasional suicidal attacks by massed Boxers.

Before very long, however, we were faced with a crisis of an entirely different nature. I managed to steal some time at the barricades each day, usually in the early evening when George took a break from our journalistic labors to dine, and had occasionally caught glimpses of Huo playing her incendiary games. (She was seen now and then by the defenders, as well, and there were numerous sermons preached by the purveyors of Western superstition within the enclave denouncing this example of Chinese superstition without! I was surprised at how easily the evidence of one's own eyes could be discounted by comforting words pronounced in a stentorian tone.)

The creature seemed to find much to amuse herself with in the capitol city. The few remaining places of Western worship were constantly inflamed (and some that had burned only halfway down in the initial conflagration were summarily ignited again). Shops that carried "foreign" goods also continued to be common targets, as were the unprotected dwellings of the "barbarians" beyond the Enclave, and any homes purported to belong to Chinese Christians (though the Boxers, remaining true to form, were as like to pronounce these such after the fact as before).

On the occasion in question Huo had directed her attentions to a group of local dwellings on the western border of the Enclave, though there was no apparent xenophobic justification for this burning and only the strategic, since they had been built near the British Legation and the fires there could presumably weaken those defenses. These burned throughout the night, however, with but little impact upon the Enclave itself.

When morning broke on the following day, though, the winds shifted and blew strongly from a northerly direction. The dying fires quickened with this breath of life, and began to lick at the Hamlin Yuan, a series of structures that surrounded the Yung Lo Ta Tien, a great library that housed innumerable irreplaceable documents relating to the history of China and its various Emperors.

This building was precariously close to the borders of the barricaded Legations, and it had been thought by the strategists within those walls that even the Boxers would quail before damaging such an illustrious site, so precious to the Chinese were their histories and the mementos of their ancestors.

Indeed the fire, when it came, was not intentional, but merely a result of Huo's greed to burn and an unlucky whim of wind. But ignite the library did, and the combination of old, dry structures and great shelves of historical fuel soon allowed it to build into an inferno. The buildings caught fire with a roar of sound, and even the trees within the compound were soon blazing like so many torches held aloft.

The danger to those under siege was immense and immediate. The walls of the British Legation were key to the defenses, and the fire could not be allowed to leap from the library to these. Thus a breach was formed in the barricades, and a muster of Royal Marines, in concert with the more daring of the civilian population, undertook a bucket brigade to challenge the flames.

Morrison of course was among those who charged to this front (and in truth I would have expected no less from him). The heat was terrible, and many lost facial hair and clothing to the furnace into which they were forced to plunge. Each new structure that ignited threw off temperatures equivalent to those of a blast furnace. Smoke blinded one and all, and as many buckets were dropped as firefighters groped forward as ever made it to the burning buildings. Worse yet, Imperial troops kept up a fusillade of rifle fire at the would-be rescuers, their own aim (if it were not intentionally high, I wondered still) confounded by the same cloak of smoke that tormented those in the bucket brigade.

I believe all would have been lost, despite the heroic efforts of the Marines and their civilian cohorts, if the winds had not shifted again and allowed the firefighters to get a leg up on the blaze. With the immediate danger to the Legation over, the mission quickly evolved from that of fire control to the rescue of the irreplaceable documents that had survived the burning. I am sorry (but not surprised, I fear) to say that this ultimately involved as much looting as salvage, and many priceless documents thus found their way into the hands of men who had little appreciation for their worth. Some of the hand-carved wooden blocks used to print the most venerable of manuscripts were themselves transported into the Legation walls, only to be used to block up holes in the barricades or to serve as playthings for children.

On a more personal level, George (who had a journalist's devotion to documents, and the older the better) had been the savoir of many pages of Chinese history, and had left these stacked beyond the reach or this or any future flames, their disposition to be decided when the siege was over. In the process, however, he had been quite badly burned, though as is often the case in times of dire need he did not notice these wounds until the crisis was over.

A woman will, of course, perceive her man's injuries before he will, particularly when they disfigure his face, and the right side of George's was horribly burned, already rising in a bubbled crop of blisters that would surely leave him unbalanced by a slick grey scar. This is not to say that I considered Morrison "mine" in any romantic sense, but I was far more susceptible to human emotion in those days, and I hope my readers can forgive that early innocence as I myself have attempted to do over the years.

At any rate I quite forgot my place and demanded that Morrison be brought to his room that I might tend to him. This was met with raised eyebrows among the others in his party, but though they would no doubt indulge themselves in rumor after the fact, my demeanor was sufficiently fierce that they granted my wish. In the room he was led to the kang and reclined there, all the while protesting that there were others more seriously hurt than he. Soon after he drifted into an exhausted sleep a minister attempted entrance, "to offer comfort," as he said, but I drove him off in a fit of fury, a solitary tract left behind in his flight.

After all had left me alone with him, his compatriots going off to alert the Enclave's physicians that they should add him to their roster of those needing attention, and the minister to lick his wounds, I slid the door shut. I did not know how much time I would have, so set to work immediately. The shock of the injuries was rapidly wearing off, and the pain was clear on George's face and in his actions, replacing his brave front with a fevered delirium. Ignoring those burns that I could not see, I held his shoulders firmly down upon the bedding and, like a cat at milk, bathed the blisters on his face with my tongue.

Barely conscious, he squirmed under these ministrations, but I used force enough to keep him immobile until I had thoroughly coated his facial burns with my own healing saliva. The effect was immediate, and by the time the doctor rapped at the door the blistering had abated and the injuries I had treated already looked far less serious than those that had not received my attention.

The physician noticed this immediately, and thus directed his efforts to the burns on Morrison's right arm and leg which, while no less horrid than the damage to his face had been, had the advantage of being invisible, no matter how badly they might scar, when clothing was worn.

I remained in the room, assisting the doctor as I could, meekly and silently passing whatever he requested as he treated the injuries with the limited remedies at hand within the Enclave. With all that could be done accomplished, he administered a dose of morphine and, with a curious glance at me, left the chamber as his patient drifted into a drugged sleep.

I remained at George's bedside as he wandered in narcotic slumber, and was uncharacteristically pleased to hear my name (or in truth Jinyu Liu's) muttered aloud as he dreamed. More satisfying still was the fact that his face was within an hour almost completely healed, while the other burns would require a long and painful recovery, and leave their calling cards upon his limbs for the rest of his life.

When I was satisfied that my risky work had borne the fruit I'd wished of it, I slipped from Morrison's chambers back to my own shared quarters. I faced questions aplenty there to be sure, but did my best to put them off by asserting that without his patronage I would likely be relegated to the Fu, and thus it was in my own interests to see that all possible care was given him. As transparent as this excuse was, it served to quiet the worst of the conjecture, and when my roommates departed to their various tasks I allowed myself a few hours of recuperative slumber.

I awoke to the tinkling of the summoning bell, shocked to realize that I had slept through the hours of darkness, a clear sign that I had more seriously depleted my energies in worry than I would have thought possible. Straightening my clothing and hair as well as I was able without either glass or comb (and giving myself a rather stern silent talking to about attachments to mortals), I hurried to Morrison's room to find him at his desk, the clothing cut from his arm and leg and the skin there heavily wrapped in gauze and looking quite uncomfortable.

"I'm told you stayed by me for some hours, Liu," he said. "I must tell you how much your concern augments whatever medication they've treated me with. The old limbs will be back to full function soon enough, I'm told. Until then I might be forced to ask you to serve as my right hand along with your other duties."

It was clear from this that George did not remember his facial burns, and thus was unaware of the magic I'd worked upon them. I sighed, my relief at his ignorance easily misunderstood for gratefulness for his being awake and upright.

"I told those in the servants' quarters that I stayed to assist the doctor out of concern for my continued employment," I told him. "I hope my actions have not compromised our secret?"

He laughed, and I took a private pleasure in the unhindered movement of the muscles beneath his good, strong face.

"I am a lodestone for rumors, my Liu," he said. "And I'm quite certain that the wagging tongues of the Enclave had been speculating lasciviously upon our relationship well before yesterday. The best lotion for gossip is inattention. There are affairs and escapades enough here to distract them in short time."

I made bold to kiss him, and he held the back of my head with his good left arm, extending the kiss until I feared he would overexcite himself.

"Not today, dearest," I whispered against his lips, gently breaking our contact. "You must heal a bit more before I would risk your health for my pleasure."

George laughed again, and this at least was healthy and strong.

"Not your pleasure alone! But you are correct, we must employ patience. Did you rest well enough to do some work today?"

It was clear that any movement of his right arm pained him, so I presumed to sort through the documents upon his desk and provide him with an oral précis of each, speaking slowly enough for George to take crabbed notes with his awkward left hand. In this way we proceeded until early afternoon, when the room grew quite stifling and he begged that we break in order to rest until the heat grew less oppressive. I left him with another kiss, and returned to the shared quarters more than happy to lay my own head down for an hour or so.

It was not to be. I had barely closed my eyes where there was a soft rapping on the sliding door. Thinking it was merely one of my roommates returning, perhaps for something forgotten in the early morning haste, I bid the supplicant come in and pulled my worn sheet up to below my eyes to signal my desire for continued sleep.

The portal slid open, and a diminutive woman entered. She was clearly Asian, and well-born, and her attire marked her as one connected to the Japanese Legation within the enclave. This would have made her visit to my quarters unusual enough, but I knew as soon as she crossed the room, by the sinuous grace of her movement, too subtle to be detected by mortal eyes, and her care to avoid what little direct sunlight invaded my quarters, that I was in the company of Kin.

Her very presence contradicted Huo's words, unless that creature had made an exception for this woman as she had for me (and I somehow suspected that Huo's indulgence did not include the Japanese, who were generally seen as the primary threat to the Qing Dynasty; regardless of the fact that the fate of the current Empire did not really seem to enter into her concerns). I had a few moments to contemplate this puzzle as the woman settled herself with infinite grace beside me.

"Why, you are so young," she said in Manchu, "just a girl like me!"

It was true, she did not have an air of great age about her, but I was still wary as I sat up, lifting the sheet with me.

"You *were* a girl, once." I dared, feeling the need to let her know that the recognition was mutual.

She giggled, it was a light and carefree sound, and teased a smile from me despite my trepidation.

"As were you," she said, "and so close in making to me that we could be sister-Kin! I would be fascinated to know how one so young came to be here in this dangerous time and this terrible place, and in such an unfortunate disguise..." My hands drifted to my face as she said this, her dark eyes sparkling. "...but alas there are other more urgent matters we must discuss."

I held my tongue and just watched her, waiting for her to continue.

"What is your name, dear?" she asked, bowing politely. "I would prefer to not continue until we are introduced, though informally."

"I am Jinyu Liu," I began, before seeing her eyebrows rise in apparent humor. "Or Paulette Monot, if you prefer."

"Oh I do prefer, most assuredly!" She replied. "Though I will publicly employ the former in honor of your subterfuge. That matter being the issue that compels my visit."

"I know," I sighed, abandoning the thin armor of the sheet and stretching. "I should not have lingered in Morrison's quarters. It was an all too human mistake."

"And a charming one. It speaks well of you I think," she said, "but that is not the matter I've come about. You healed him, Miss Jinyu, you performed a miracle in these most superstition-haunted times."

"No one was there," I protested, feeling the dread rising in me like a slow fever. "We were alone when I did so."

She tittered again, but it was more rueful than joyous.

"Did you not think that there were others in the fire with him, that those who helped him out of the conflagration would have noticed so disfiguring an injury?" She shook her head in approbation. "When one of those individuals encounters him, and perceives his face all whole while his arm and leg are bandaged, the tales will fly, and they will flutter towards you, Liu-who-is-Paulette."

I was ashamed that I had not considered this, but had acted out of impulse rather than logic, a weakness that I vowed would pass with the years. In order to buy time to consider my options, I questioned her again.

"How is it that you know of this?" I asked.

"There are benefits to being small and Asian," she said. "To most Westerners we are all but indistinguishable, and I can often move unseen where others might be noticed. Thus I was unobserved when the firefighters returned. I saw his injuries and saw *you* see them, knowing of course at once what you were. The look on your dear face predicted what was to come. And now you have confirmed it. I am, by the way, known as Wakahisa Miho, but please call me by my given name."

"Then tell me, Miho," I said, "what of Huo?" The question had been nagging me since her appearance.

She held a shushing finger to her mouth, looking from side to side as if fearful that we might be overheard, though her expression was exaggerated and theatrical rather than truly concerned.

"Huo," she said, her pretty face twisted into a moue of distaste. "Of course you would have encountered her. I'm surprised that she has not driven you away or worse. I, however, even that creature's fiery eyes cannot detect. But we will discuss that at another time. Our current concerns lie with you. Whatever am I to do with you, Paulette Monot?"

The fears that had earlier subsided sprang up again in full force, and I readied myself for conflict. I answered carefully.

"You can do nothing with me that I do not allow, Wakahisa Miho, surely you must know that."

She studied me thoughtfully, and I knew she was aware of the tensing of my muscles, the sharpening of my senses.

"The language we speak in is neither yours nor mine, Paulette, so perhaps my words were spoken or heard in error. We could sit here all day and compare the length of our teeth, perhaps, but that would do nothing to assure your safety."

I deflated as quickly as I had angered.

"I'm sorry," I said. "That was uncalled for. I seem to have let fatigue and emotion interfere with my thinking."

Miho touched my shoulder with a delicate hand, I barely felt its weight, but somehow the contact with another Kin sent a wave of relief through me that I could not explain.

"My elders tell me I will outgrow the same failings in time. I'm sure that will be the case with you, as well," she said.

"Are they here?" I asked, the thought of strength in Kindred numbers somehow quite attractive at the moment.

"Oh no, no. Only me. If we were many Huo might know, and my Patron would not countenance such in any case. But to the matter at hand," she drew her arm back, a dance in the smallest turn of her wrist, and tallied off points on raised fingers; "Morrison cannot be unhealed, and I doubt you would accede to that were it possible. His unnatural recovery will be noticed, it is only a matter of time. When it has been so suspicion will fall upon you. I believe you must leave here, Paulette-Liu, and the more quickly the better."

My heart sank at the thought. It seemed as if my life had been nothing but flight of late, and I am not a woman who finds fleeing natural. I countered by counting off a few items of my own.

"I was among the Red Lanterns before, and cannot return to them. I have...an enemy there now. The Dowager, for all I know, still thinks Jinyu Liu is in her prison. And I do not know the limits of Huo's reprieve."

Miho laughed behind both hands; as was every movement she made, it was a tiny piece of theater perfectly performed.

"You have been busy for such a girl!" She said. "Perhaps there is an alternative, then. But I believe we must think of it quickly. If only we could direct the suspicion elsewhere."

I spoke before the thought was completed, and let it crystallize around my words as they came.

"The Lanterns profess healing abilities, but surely their superstitions are no more onerous than those held within these walls. Is there not anyone within the Legations who would glory in such a reputation?"

As the small churches burned and those in them fled the Boxers for the relative security of the Enclave compound, it had become perhaps the most preached-at community in the world, Self-professed Word-bringers of all denominations clashed within its barricades, many of them distraught and at their wit's end as a result of the horrors they had experienced. Surely, I thought, there must be among them one or more who would grasp at evidence of a miraculous healing to buoy up his (for they were a strictly male lot, an argument I would venture against their legitimacy) reputation. At the end of that train of thought I found a caboose in the form of the minister who'd fled before my anger in Morrison's quarters.

From that thought to a plan was the work of mere moments. I outlined my proposal to Miho, who seemed surprised and pleased by the depths of my deviousness. Haste was imperative, though, so we agreed upon a later meeting date and I fled toward George's quarters, careful to remain unseen as I did so, and she returned to her own section of the Enclave.

Morrison was still asleep as I crept in, trauma and heat doping him as surely as had the morphine. I quickly located the tract that had been dropped in the minister's flight, and a glance at it told me that luck was with me. Roughly printed, and in a crude translation of the Chinese documents used to proselytize to the masses, it was titled "Healing Powers of God," or some such, and had likely been prepared for teaching English to the converts. The Chinese (and for all I knew the Christian teachers themselves) held these things to be something like magic incantations, to be read in order to obtain the blessings promised within.

George, like many of those who make their living with words, had a habit of reading any print that found its way to hand, be it book or letter or label on a packet of patent medicine. Counting on this peccadillo, I placed the tract next to his sleeping form on the kang and slipped out of his room to resume my nap.

As I soon learned (for when food is short it seems rumor steps up to quiet the empty stomachs) my plan worked better than I could have wished. It happened that George's physician had visited him just before I returned for our afternoon's work, and had brought with him a comrade who had also participated in the bucket brigade. They had discovered Morrison propped up on a pair of pillows and perusing the tract. His compatriot had seen the state of the patient's once-burned face and the supposedly holy paper and fallen to his knees then and there. George, who remembered nothing of such injuries, pooh-poohed it all, but the tale spread and was soon the talk of the Enclave.

It reached the Japanese legation certainly, as I learned when next Miho and I managed an assignation. We had contrived to meet in one of the yards, ostensibly repairing the barricades there, that being a form of labor that involved Legation personnel and converts alike.

"The ruse was prettily done, Paulette," she offered while helping me shift a bullet-torn couch back into position, both of us careful to make the chore look as difficult as it should. "The Legation is abuzz with the tale, and the tract-bearing Reverend Duerr is reportedly the envy of the Protestant community. Those Catholics who aren't huddled with Bishop Favier in the Peitang Cathedral" (a site separate from the Legation per se, and also under siege) "are furiously jealous, and whispering darkly of blasphemy."

"So," I replied, lowering my end of the piece of furniture back into place, making a flimsy wall for our riflemen to hide behind, and speaking English as she had, "I have bought some time, but we both know that it is not infinite. Perhaps here, in the eye of the storm as it were, we can spare a moment for you to tell me how it is that Huo cannot detect you."

She studied me carefully.

"Well," Miho said, "I suppose if you were in the creature's thrall you would already have told her about my presence, which would do nothing but infuriate her since I would remain undetectable. So, and I do not mean to insult you with my hesitation, I suppose there is no risk in telling you more."

Perhaps it is because I had been long without the company of Kin, but I found my pride very easily pricked.

"Tell me what you will and hide from me what you wish, Miss Wakahisa. I shall not beg," I said.

This outburst quite shocked here, and brought her hand to her mouth in what I was beginning to learn was a characteristic gesture.

"Don't allow yourself to be cruel," she said, "It is not becoming. I shall trust you, and if you allow yourself to do the same you might find you have made a very dear friend."

I calmed myself before answering, aware that I had not been acting rationally.

"That I will do, then, Miho, and hope that I learn to appreciate the value of such a wise sister."

Where there had been clouds on her delicate features, the sun rose as quickly.

"Then I shall tell you all," she said. And I composed myself to listen.

"You must already know that the creature Huo is old," she began, "as ancient as the most venerable of our Kind, if not older still. She, and I use that pronoun only because it suits the form the creature now inhabits, is of the fires beneath the soil and rock of this land rather than of the Empire, and none know when and how she came into being. Such young things as you or I are helpless before her."

"And yet she cannot determine your nature," I prodded.

Miho grinned at me, a coy, teasing little smile.

"When you have spoken with Huo, did she make mention of an ancient creature of another sort?"

I puzzled over this for a moment before remembering a scrap of conversation.

"She could not tell me precisely what she was," I ventured, "but she did say that she was not a dragon."

Miho applauded as if I were a prize pupil conjugating a Latin verb.

"Yes!" She said. "It is what she is not, and it is the thing that can confound her."

"A dragon?" I said, all at sea, "what has such mythology to do with your concealment?"

"A myth is only a segment of a reality that is not yet understood," she pronounced almost primly. "Are the Kin not regarded as mere fantasy by many of the Great Thinkers of the mortal world?"

I allowed that this was true, already suspecting where she was leading but quite unwilling to go there on my own.

"Here there be dragons," she said playfully, "and in my homeland as well."

I had, since my transformation, been forced to admit that there were more things in heaven and earth than were dreamt of in mortal philosophy, but this was a further leap indeed.

"Assuming that I accept the existence of such creatures," I said, tentatively feeling my way, "what part would their presence play in your ability to confound Huo's senses?"

"She is a thing of fire, as you certainly know," Miho said. "And contrary to what you might have been led to believe by Western legend, the dragons of the Orient are beasts of water, which is a wall that flames cannot cross."

I glanced at the sky despite myself.

"But there is no such beast hovering above you," I said.

Miho frowned, as if attempting to wring out the correct words to explain what she wished.

"It need not be with me externally, dear Paulette, for it is with me always. The dragon is within me."

It was clear that I was going to need additional information, and I indicated such to her.

"We call it Watatsumi," she began, "though like Huo and, I think, all of the ancient ones, it answers to numerous names, as many as the creatures that have come after it have fashioned in their attempts to capture it in their understanding. When the first of the Kin arose in my country (and that is another story complex and confused by the years), they encountered it and were overtaken with awe. Watatsumi saw this, and because of the respect they demonstrated it treated them kindly.

"As the ages passed, the dragon became weary. The mortals bred like rats and covered the land. They prayed to the creature incessantly, so that their praise became stale and even their worshipful sacrifices became tedious things. Eventually it fled beneath the waters, there to perform its given tasks in sweet solitude. But it did not forget the Kin who had treated it with the honor due it and asked little in return. We call upon it in only times of great need, but when we do so Watatsumi still answers."

I threw myself down on the couch we'd positioned, releasing a small cloud of dust and a few spent projectiles that had been trapped in its upholstery. It was all rather much to absorb.

"And so you called upon this dragon, this Watatsumi, and what did you ask of it?"

"It is called "the Dragon's Kiss..." she began.

I suppose I was not quite finished with my bout of prickliness, because here I interjected.

"I am counted as being quite liberal in my approach to romance," I said, "but surely there are difficulties of scale involved?"

Miho rolled her eyes at my interruption (and likely at the horrible if unintentional English pun contained therein) but soldiered onward.

"It is called the Dragon's Kiss," she repeated, daring me with a glance to speak again, "It is not a literal kissing, but the partaking of a single drop of blood from a wound, made by the creature itself, piercing the relatively thin skin beneath its wings. I am not one of the scientists included among the Kin, but as I understand it the ichor from the dragon binds with the blood within us and leaves us seeming, to such as Huo at least, neither fish nor fowl as it were."

I studied the girl carefully, looking for any evidence of draconian transformation, but saw none. Miho resembled nothing but a petite and lovely young woman.

"Is it permanent, then? Will you always have this thing inside you?"

"The effect is quite persistent," she said, "particularly given the usually glacial change of cells within such as us. If I were to be seriously wounded and have to heal, however, the creation of new flesh would speed the dilution of the ichor dramatically. Fortunately I've been able to avoid such misadventures during my time here."

"And why exactly are you here," I persisted. "Simply to observe? Certainly there would be easier ways to obtain information from within the Delegations. I know that your country has designs upon China, and is ready to swoop in should the Dowager falter. Do you seek to further such plans? "

"I do not serve Japan here, dear," Miho was emphatic in this denial, "but only my Kin. The Elders among us believe that, should China open up to our kind, it would provide the opportunity to swell our ranks, and several of those long denied the blessing of creating children would thus be granted the opportunity."

"For that to happen, would you not have to find a way to permanently confound Huo?"

"Both Huo and the Empire must fall for our ascendance," she replied. "There are other forces in China we would be hesitant to challenge, but should the Qing fail, it is believed that all of those, including this country's own dragons, would fall into deeper slumber and cease to resist us. It is likely only because you have earned Huo's tolerance that you have not encountered worse than her in this land already."

I shivered involuntarily.

"Worse than Huo I cannot, or do not choose to, imagine," I said. "But if the Empire falls and China is divided up among the powers, would not the Kin that dwell in those lands determine the future here. Surely your nation would not hope to take the lion's share of the spoils."

She shrugged.

"The seats of the Powers are distant. I am not a mistress of geopolitics, though, dear Paulette, but only a soldier charged with a mission, even as I believe are you?"

As forthright as Miho had been, I was not yet ready to return the favor, so I answered equivocally.

"Regardless, dear Miho, it seems we are on opposite sides of the coin for the moment. You have your Dragon's Kiss and I, all unwilling, the patronage of the creature Huo."

"But we are sister-Kin," she replied, "which surely trumps both of those factors in our loyalties. So let us learn to be friends and, should our objectives at any point intersect, consider such allegiance as would be appropriate."

I could not but smile at this, and shook her hand in the Western manner. This action she found humorous, or titillating, or both, but she squeezed mine in turn and some sort of pact was sealed.

So it was that we dispensed with talk of the Great Game and the small parts we might be called upon to play within it, and spent the rest of that evening seemingly busy upon the barricades. While we worked, however, we spoke of more intimate things; our pasts and our makings, our hopes and our dreams and our fears.

By the time we were forced to part to tend to other obligations, Miho to return to her Delegation and I to look in upon Morrison before he settled in for his night's repose, we had left all thought of mission and its potential conflicts behind us, and had birthed a friendship that I cherish to this day, and that I would have reason to be thankful for again in the near future.

Chapter Fourteen

As time passed, the situation within the Enclave was desperate and hopeful by turns, as news from the Forbidden City would at one moment indicate support for the Westerners and at the next seem to be flogging the army to kill them one and all. It was unclear whether the Dowager Empress was hopelessly confused and vacillating or a devious mistress of tactics. I only knew that, from the brief time I spent in Cixi's company, she may not have complete control over her court but was not likely to long remain confused.

This uncertainty came to a head late in June. My George (I've said it again, oh how quickly we slip into the foolishness of possession!) was well on the mend, due as much no doubt to a strong constitution as to whatever poor cures were available to the physicians at hand. He was well enough to participate in a series of small raids aimed at rescuing a few of the Chinese Christians not already within our walls, and these actions on the part of the Delegations seemed to spur the Imperial troops to greater efforts of their own.

In the midst of this escalation came a strange message, purportedly from the Empress herself. From what I was able to gather (since I was unable to see the official document itself; and even George had to be satisfied with a summation), it apologized to the ladies of the Enclave for any inconveniences (?) the recent unpleasantness had caused, bemoaned that events had delayed their removal to cooler summer quarters, and assured one and all that the "ruffians" would soon be dealt with. More to the point, a second document delivered soon thereafter suggested that all of the residents of the Enclave, with their staff and guards, would be advised to leave the barricades on the following morning and, under the protection of the Imperial army, proceed to Tientsin, as the Chinese government could no longer assure their safely in Pekin.

This occasioned a great debate among the besieged, with the more timid inclined to believe in the promise of security and take the offer and the hope it implied (though of course none of us knew the situation in Tientsin at that time, George's message bearer not yet having returned). A minority, which included Morrison and Sir Claude MacDonald (head of the British delegation and in George's mind at least, a good man if hidebound), predicted that the army would fall upon any so putting themselves within its power and slaughter them to a man.

The debate was bitter and contentious, with cruel words flung by those on both sides. In the end, over the obstacles of language and temperament a compromise was forged. The evacuation proposal was to be accepted "in principle," but with a demand for a further meeting with a representative of the Empire on the designated morning, purportedly to arrange the logistics of and timing for the retreat. Perhaps this amounted to nothing more than kicking the stone down the road, but it at least put the matter to a temporary rest.

And there it remained when Miho captured me on one of my perambulations between my room and Morrison's quarters. She took me by the arm with a laugh, and led me, all lighthearted it seemed, into the relative security of an empty yard. (You might think that others in the compound would have been suspicious of us, Japan being China's great enemy, but such is the nature of prejudice that I think the Westerners to a man just sniffed and dismissed our *tête-a-têtes* as "demn furrin bizness," and let it go at that). There, away from curious ears (if there were any such concerned with our Asian women-talk) my friend's demeanor became far more serious, and she fairly hissed out her words.

"It is a trap, Paulette, surely you see this," she said without preamble. "When they are beyond the barricades the troops will turn on them and slaughter one and all." (It being assumed by both her and me without a word being spoken that, however dire the circumstances, we would be able to escape the massacre.)

"Of course," I relied. "Morrison maintains the same, but the fainter hearts among the Delegations are willing to grasp at any straw that offers closure to their ordeal."

"If this occurs," my friend said slyly, for she had certainly uncovered my mission regardless of my silence on the matter "you know it will provide the excuse the Powers are seeking to smash the Qing once and for all."

I had considered the same, but with my preoccupation with caring for George, and providing what pleasure I could to us both in his still delicate state, I had admittedly not let the implications for my objectives strike home.

"All will turn on the meeting with the representative from the Forbidden City," I replied. "There is still hope, I think, that more cautious minds will prevail."

Miho smiled sweetly.

"Indeed, that is the point upon which the future will depend. I suspect the Qing will not be of a mood to entertain a lengthy delay. We must be ready, you and I, for whatever outcome might result."

I nodded my agreement, but I was already thinking to the future, and wondering how I might at this time place my thumb upon the scales of history and make them tilt in the direction Lady Ellen desired.

"The meeting is scheduled for nine a.m.," I eventually replied. "Perhaps we should observe it, in order to steal a march upon whatever might result." After some further discussion, this we agreed to do.

Thus Miho and I were peering from a vantage point within the barricades as the assembled delegates awaited the Qing's reply. The event did not go as assumed, however, and no response from the Empire came. After waiting for only thirty minutes, Baron von Ketteler of the German Delegation, a rash and excitable man, could take no more. He announced that he would himself go to meet with the Mandarins, and "wait...if I have to sit there all night." Several, including George, attempted to dissuade him, but he was resolute, and prepared to depart in his official chair, accompanied by his Delegation's Chinese secretary (since the Baron himself spoke no language other than his own).

Telling my friend that we would learn little until the German's return, I bade her adieu and hurried back to my quarters.

Taking advantage of the privacy of the shared room, however tenuous, I refreshed my eye drops and made my way to the barricades. In the current state of uncertainty about the intentions of the Qing, that border had become somewhat porous (witness von Ketteler's rash decision to venture out). Where once any Oriental not in Boxer or Red Lantern garb had been assumed to be Christian and persecuted as such, it was now not a rare thing for the Chinese from within the Enclave to slip out in an attempt to purchase foodstuffs from the few remaining purveyors who were willing to risk selling to anyone who possessed the correct number of coins.

Thus I dared sneak out myself and, clad in my blue, hurry ahead of the German's palanquin, My plan was ill formed. I was only certain that I must somehow prevent the evacuation and probable slaughter of the Delegations, which as Miho foretold would bring the full wrath of the Powers down upon the Qing and likely result in the end of the Empire and the partition of China; a consummation which would be contrary to my Mistress's wishes.

I passed the carried chair at a safe distance, but close enough to see that the German was savoring a cigar and reading as he was purveyed along, the smoke from the former giving his palanquin the appearance of a small steam engine chugging through the mass of people surrounding it. The arrogance of this action was palpable, and could serve as an arrow for my quiver. I would, I decided, try to turn the crowd against him and thus drive him back to the Enclave. Failing in this, I confess that I planned to kill him myself and lay the blame upon the insurgents or the Empire itself.

Positioning myself in von Ketteler's path, I contemplated possible courses of action. I could, I thought, spread the rumor that he was armed and planned to assassinate the Empress, or perhaps that he carried a humiliating ultimatum from his government to the Qing. I scanned the crowd around me looking for the more suggestible of the Boxers nearby, and was prepared to begin my strategy of disinformation when I heard the sounds of an altercation.

Hurrying to the site of the disturbance, I found the German in the center of an angry crowd. He had abandoned his chair (and it seemed it had abandoned him, his porters and Chinese translator were nowhere to be seen). I could only assume that he was responding to some perceived insult, for he was standing over a young Chinese, the latter already driven to his knees, and belaboring the unfortunate individual with his walking stick.

As I watched, uncertain as to where and how to intercede, von Ketteler freed his holstered pistol and fired a shot into the air, presumably to intimidate and drive back the crowd that was now pressing him closely. This action had an effect opposite to that intended, however, as the sound of the gun drew more Chinese toward the scuffle, and the masses fed upon their own anger until the German was surrounded by a shrieking mob. He fired several more shots, whether again into the air or at his attackers I could not tell, and I was on the verge of pushing forward to his rescue, illogically and at the risk of my disguise, when I saw the flash of sunlight upon a sword blade and knew that any aid I could provide would be too late to save him.

It was as if the crowd had become maddened by the smell of blood (which I confess tickled my nose enticingly), and the German, now certainly dead, was lost to my sight beneath a flailing of fists and feet and sticks and steel. Somewhat sobered by what I had seen, I abandoned any thought of intercession and made my way back to the Enclave, slipping in through the same barricade by which I'd exited, to wait for another to bring the news of von Ketteler's murder.

I rejoined Morrison in his room, he not surprised at my lateness given the disrupted state of affairs in the Legations resulting from the Qing's ultimatum and the resulting uncertainty. We were barely beginning to decipher the second document when another of his servants burst in breathless, bearing the information that the German had been killed, presumably with the compliance of the Empire. With this shocking event all support for evacuation under the supposed protection of the Imperial army evaporated, and those in the Legations determined to hold fast and wait for rescue, whether from Seymour's forces or those in Tientsin, from both of whom no word had been heard for some time.

It was not too many days before this cloud of ignorance was lifted with the return of Morrison's messenger, Jie. He slipped back into the Delegation compound in the early hours of the morning, little the worse for wear save innumerable bug bites and a touch of heat exhaustion, having survived questioning by the Imperial army and Boxers alike. It was only his mention of a relative in a nearby village that saved him from the latter, since the man he referred to was well known and this small slice of truth proved large enough to cover the greater lie of Jie's innocence.

The news that he brought was perhaps not what my companions under siege would have hoped, but it was at least accurate information, and not without its hopeful aspects. Seymour's relief expedition, which, as we know, had been stranded between Tientsin and Pekin by Boxers who destroyed the railway tracks both in front of and behind the forces, had been obligated to retreat back toward the town from which it had departed.

Nursing many wounded and short of both food and ammunition, the force had chanced upon the Hsiku Arsenal complex, a multi-acre installation of which it had been quite ignorant. Capturing this fortress (while sustaining heavy losses), Seymour found within it stores of rice and ammunition and had been able to hold that ground until newly arrived troops from Tientsin had arrived to relieve the relievers; after which all had returned to that town, now being steadily reinforced with a trickle of multi-national soldiers and sailors from the coast.

So while our hopes for an immediate reprieve by Seymour's expedition were dashed, those in the Legations were buoyed by the knowledge that Tientsin was holding out and strengthened, and that the forces there were now aware that the Pekin Delegation was intact but in dire need of aid. This information, on the heels of von Ketteler's assassination, stiffened the resolve of all within the Enclave and convinced them to hold on in the face of whatever the Qing and Boxers might send against them.

Chapter Fifteen

A diet of horse meat and rice might not be the menu of choice of the discriminating gourmand, but I can attest that it has no deleterious effects upon the libido of the mortal male. With his burns now healing rapidly, George was once more capable of a wide range of movement, and like a child who has first been exposed to sweets and as a consequence does not want to eat anything else, he was quite single-minded and voracious.

As often as not, I'd arrive at his quarters in the morning to find him still abed on the kang, for the most part undressed, and holding his arms out to me in silent appeal. As, during his recuperation, I had taken pains to assure his pleasure, often with little concern for my own, I was determined to turn his passions to my advantage.

On one such morning, therefore, I arrived to find him still reclining. Sliding and latching the door shut (though barring a crisis none would venture to open it without first knocking and being bade enter), I slipped out of my simple clothing;

but rather than approach him immediately, I locked my eyes upon his and began touching myself.

I squeezed each breast, voicing small murmurs of pleasure as I did, and pinched and pulled at my nipples until they were erect and sensitized. He squirmed beneath the thin sheet covering his lower self and begged me to approach, but I did not move one step toward him.

Instead, I trailed my fingertips across my stomach, nails leaving thin white lines on my tan skin. Then, taking a wider stance and rocking my pelvis toward him, I touched myself below, tracing between the petals of my sex from bottom to top, opening the pink leaves there and letting him see the glisten of their wetness.

With my eyes half closed, I worried at my clitoris with a fingertip, circling it and flicking at it, all with the appropriate vocal accompaniment. He slipped a hand beneath the cotton to touch himself, and I smiled around a low moan, dipping first one finger and then two between the lips of my sex and deep within, slowly working my hand to drive them in and draw them out, and rocking my hips in concert.

George was quite beside himself by this point, and reached for me again, croaking "Please..." in a rough voice. Still I did not approach, but slowly withdrew my fingers, spreading them so he could see the strands of wet stretch and break between them, and then slipped them into my mouth, licking and suckling each one slowly.

My lover was by this time quite frantic with desire, but I had an agenda of my own. I approached him finally, walking slowly to let him admire the soft swing of my breasts and the shine of wetness below. When I came within reach, he grabbed for my hips and attempted to pull me down onto the kang, but I resisted (using a bit more strength than might be expected, and counting upon his lust to allow him to ignore this), brushing his hands away and instead taking his head between my palms.

George looked up at me, confused, and I smiled down at him and gently brought his face against my stomach. He kissed me there, exploring my navel with his tongue, and while he was busy at that I guided his head lower. He resisted but for a fraction of a second, this being something new to him I think, and not necessarily in the repertoire of the Victorian male, but ultimately allowed himself to be maneuvered, and touched a tentative tongue to the wet flower I had thus offered him.

My moan was not feigned this time, and my hands on his head grew more insistent. It was, I think, the voicing of my pleasure that freed him from any last misgivings, and he busied himself with lips and teeth and tongue, forcing the latter deep within me with darting strokes, and slicking his face with my wetness. If he was yet to be surprised to find me cool where another woman would be warm, he gave no sign, and I rocked with his attentions until I could take no more and fell to the kang beside him, legs spread and ready for what was to be a rapid consummation, but only the first of several.

In this way, day by day I expanded our repertoire, and found my darling to be a willing and precocious pupil, to the point that I occasionally had to be quite insistent or we would have gotten no work done at all. This could not be allowed to happen, as I believed that his reportage of the historic events surrounding us would be as important (or at least entertaining) to his people as I hope this account might be to the Kin. Furthermore, should no evidence of our reportorial collaboration be produced, it might have set tongues again to wagging in a manner that would be pleasing to neither of us.

But tongues will wag, regardless of the motivation, and all the more so in the Petri plate of an imprisoned society. Jealousy will add its motivation, as well, and I was aware that a number of the Legation wives (both those who had been erroneously linked with Morrison already and those who had not yet shared that distinction) kept a covetous eye on the man counted as the most eligible bachelor in the compound. In short order such rumor-mongering plunged me into a situation that I could not abide. As had been the case in the past, I owed what warning I received to the ever-open ears of the inestimable Miho.

She captured me as I was returning from the laundry, where I had volunteered for a shift in addition for my "work" with Morrison in order to better disappear into the army of faceless Chinese who kept life within the Delegations running in a more or less orderly fashion. Miho glanced at my hands, clucked her tongue as if at the damage they'd sustained (when of course there was none), and led me into an empty alcove.

I had not discussed my amorous adventures with my friend, but I was not fool enough to believe that she was ignorant of them. Her senses were, after all, fully the equal of my own. So she proceeded without preamble, assuming my understanding that she knew all of my so-called secrets.

"Notorious and open lewdness," she announced as soon as we were safe from curious ears, "would, I've learned, seem to be an actionable offense still under British law. Apparently the simple fornication and even miscegenation laws have fallen off the books since the demise of the Puritans."

I eyed my friend curiously.

"And this concerns me how?" I asked.

"Tales told below stairs are oft repeated above," Miho continued, "and even closed doors are thin. Morrison is a man, and thus vulnerable to female wiles, especially the whispered-about erotic mysteries of an Eastern woman. In short, dear Paulette, he is to be saved from himself, and from you."

"By whom," I demanded, bristling. I had all too often had to play the victim during this mission, and I admit my patience with the role was wearing thin. "There are ways enough to die in this Enclave, and my imagination is both quick and wide ranging."

Miho laughed through her fingers.

"Your imagination, dear one, would seem to be at the root of your troubles. Now calm yourself and listen to me.

"It seems that one lady in particular, a matron of unchallenged probity and perhaps repression to match, has heard tales of what transpires in the room in which you labor daily, and brought them to a man of the cloth whose reputation has blossomed, ironically as a result of your own machinations."

"Duerr?" I could scarcely believe it.

"One and the same," she answered, shaking her head at the wonder of it all, "he proposes to conduct an inquiry into your actions, an investigation that could have far-seeing consequences."

"George will not allow it." I said, furious to even pretend that I needed a champion, though if I hoped to maintain my ruse I most certainly did.

"Ah," Miho countered, "but the minister is but a tool of Lady MacDonald, and it is not a great leap from there to the ear of Sir Claude. Mr. Morrison may well be a man of stellar reputation, and an individual who does not suffer fools gladly, but he is without any real authority in this place."

"Be that as it may, my dear friend," I said, "I am weary of being hounded from pillar to post. They have nothing but tales told out of school, innuendo and worse. There are such stories spread about many here, perhaps if I were to give all of these a public airing the wind would go out of this prosecution?"

Miho sighed.

"You are impetuous, sweet Paulette, perhaps it is why so many find you charming?" She teased me with her eyes. "But if you insist upon taking this route, I will do what I can to find those among the Enclave's servants who would willingly testify to other tales on indiscretion."

From that point, the situation accelerated rapidly. Morrison was well aware of it when we next met, and characteristically showed little concern for his own reputation and much for mine. When I had assured him of my resolve to go forward, and explained my plans to muddy the water with evidence of the breadth of rumor constantly circulating in the Legations, he reluctantly agreed, but posed a caveat of his own.

"If you do this, Liu, you must only speak in Chinese when questioned," he advised. "The rapidity of your growing facility in English could be seen as a point of suspicion."

I readily agreed to this, thinking that it would give me an invisible advantage as I would be able to judge the accuracy of the translations provided to my judges, and correct these if necessary.

I was formally made aware of the charges the following day, and accepted the summons with what I felt was appropriate meekness. Meanwhile, the diligent Miho had recruited a half score of witnesses willing to expound on rumors pertaining to those other than me, including several of the leading lights of the international assembly who were said to have frequently visited courtesans before the uprising made such sport too risky.

The "inquiry," for such it had been designated, was held in the British Delegation, with the full spectrum of international Delegates in attendance and the recently renowned Reverend Duerr assigned the task of interlocutor. It was immediately clear that many in this audience regarded the affair as a waste of time that could be better used seeing to the defenses (or at the very least managing the more essential rationing of spirits), and I confess that I began the ordeal with optimism.

My mood was improved still when, as Duerr (pandering to the Delegates with a flurry of "my Lords") began his opening remarks, he was immediately interrupted by the French Delegate, M. Stephen Pichon.

"I think I speak for many," he intoned, using French that was translated for the rest of the ministers, a pitiful few of whom spoke the languages of their compatriots, "when I call for a dismissal of this foolishness. We are besieged! Our very lives are endangered! Is this a time to squander our attention upon a ribald farce such as this?"

Duerr was quick to reply. Standing, his air an uneasy blend of obsequiousness and arrogance, he addressed the assembly.

"It would perhaps, my Lords, not be the time to dwell upon such indiscretions as those we originally gathered to hear, however abhorrent they might be to civilized men...and ladies" (the latter he added, I'm sure, to remind the judges that the minister had worked diligently to gain the support of their wives). But matters have since evolved, and I believe it is a far more dangerous question that my Lords will have to rule upon today, surpassing whatever foibles might take place around us," he continued, swelling perceptibly as he spoke, "for I have evidence that the woman known as Jinyu Liu is not what she appears to be!"

Chapter Sixteen

Duerr's remarks ignited a rumbling of puzzlement from the assembled dignitaries. I awaited the translation into Chinese to react, and even then only betrayed confusion. All the while, though, my mind was racing. A glance at Miho, seated in the back of the Japanese section, told me that she shared my surprise and concern, but that I would be alone in any reaction, as to reveal herself would not only cost her a seat at the tables of power but perhaps ultimately alert Huo to her hidden presence as well.

Though I maintained every outward appearance of calm, my sinews were taut as bowstrings. When the evidence, whatever it might be, was presented, I would have only seconds to decide whether it was susceptible to challenge and, if not, to flee, harming only as many as necessary of these men upon whose continued resolve Lady Ellen's hopes rested.

With the aplomb of a showman (which, indeed, all of his calling are to a point), the German minister reached behind the desk that served as his improvised podium and produced my bedroll. Miho looked puzzled at this revelation, and I myself wondered where it might lead. The unmasking that I had most feared was not to be, it seemed, but I was for the moment at a loss to predict what was to come; my eye drops being secreted, as they had been since my earlier mistake, upon my person.

My Recording Device and pepper-box were of course among the effects in the roll, and since such things were unlikely to be in the possession of a village girl, I thought myself in danger of being accused of thievery, or even of the former item being viewed as a bomb or some other sort of infernal weapon. At least the Device was bereft of recording coils, as these I had also removed for safe keeping and rolled up in my sash. Thus I busied myself with developing possible counters to any accusation as I awaited Duerr's revelation.

Before the minister could proceed, however, George stood, his face flushed with anger, and shouted.

"Is there no respect for private property here, then? Have we so cast aside the trappings of civilization that we might so violate a lady's personal possessions?"

In reply Duerr undid the ropes holding my roll together, unfurled the worn blanket that I had used since beginning my adventure, and held up a distinctive short-sleeved crimson blouse.

"A lady," he asked in sonorous tones, "or perhaps a Red Lantern?"

The dignitaries erupted in a Babel of multilingual comment, and a glance at George showed me that even he was shocked by the revelation. Maintaining a look of innocent confusion, I took stock of my situation. None of the Delegates were armed (which struck me as strange given our state of siege), but it was likely that there were pistols among the onlookers, and two guards stood at the door, both veterans of many a firefight with the Boxers and bristling with weaponry.

Seeming to gather himself, and riding roughshod over the doubts that surely plagued him, Morrison spoke up again.

"It is a piece of clothing, nothing more. Jinyu Liu arrived among us wearing only the garments that she appears in before you. Is it surprising that one with so little might be moved to steal a perfectly functional blouse, or even to slip it from a corpse?"

MacDonald nodded at this interjection, and addressed his first question directly at me.

"So tell us, Miss Jinyu, how did you come by this shirt?"

I dutifully awaited translation, surreptitiously noting the locations of my potential adversaries, and when it had been given me spoke in a small voice.

"I thought it pretty." I said.

"Yes, yes," MacDonald replied. "Pretty, yes, but we need to know where you got it, you see?"

Again I took advantage of the delay in translation to plan my reply.

"A dead girl," I said, haltingly. "She did not need it. I thought the short sleeves would be pretty on my arms?"

There were a few knowing chuckles at this reply, and Morrison hid his face in his hands briefly.

Duerr laughed too, and then addressed me directly.

"Tell us Miss Jinyu, if that is indeed your name, do you believe you can fly? Are you able to start fires with the flutter of a fan? Can you enable miraculous healing?"

"I have not tried any of those things," I replied, "but the people say that you healed George Morrison with your Christian magic."

This reply brought laughter from many in the room, but I was certain my troubles were not yet over.

"I did not heal him," the minister thundered, doing his level best to appear scandalized, "it was the Lord's doing!"

"Then why please," I answered softly, my eyes down, "are you questioning me here and not Him?"

I could see Duerr's color rise at this, but he fought for control and mastered his fury. This was his moment in the sun, after all, and he was determined to shine. At the same time, I knew I could perhaps delay matters with such banter, but the end result nonetheless looked to be unfavorable to me. Miho was still watching, her delicate face as blank of expression as a porcelain doll now, and Morrison looked angry, though I feared as much at his own nagging doubts as at the machinations of the German minister.

The latter, in fact, only shook his head ruefully at my barb.

"See, my Lords," he said, "see how clever she is, and as agile as a serpent. Qualities far more likely to be found in a spy than in a destitute villager, are they not?"

When the translation was complete, I replied, my voice again appropriately subdued.

"I see. So when a Chinese woman shows signs of wit, she can only be a she-devil?" I asked.

Duerr ran his hands through his hair, which was thin and left his fingers slick with whatever vile pomade he'd dressed it with.

"Yessssss," he hissed the word, bending his neck toward where I stood, seemingly helpless. "Yes the woman who calls herself Jinyu Liu is clever as a viper, I suspect she still believes that she can twist and twine her way out of this pickle with downcast eyes and words soft spoken to belie the venom in them.

"Even were I to produce the work that she and Morrison have accomplished," and here he cut his eyes to the Ladies that were massed in the back of the room, "in whatever time they could spare for such things; even if you could see for your own eyes how her understanding of English and Manchu blossomed so rapidly, to the point that she was actually composing messages in the former; even then I fear she might turn your heads."

I heard skeptical muttering from the assembled delegates, and dared to believe that the Reverend's performance was losing their attention for a second time. My adversary must have noticed the same, however, for he proceeded quickly to the second of his revelations.

"My Lords," he began again, "you might forgive the lasciviousness and the rumors of unnatural acts; you might overlook her unlikely intelligence and seemingly unnatural language skills; perhaps some of you might even attempt to explain away the damning red blouse so carefully hidden away among her private things. But even the most gentle and forgiving of you, even he who would prefer to *not* throw even the last stone but would let it fall from his fingers unflung, even he must give credence to a witness!

I glanced at Miho again, who answered with a tiny head shake; even her enviable below-stairs intelligence apparatus had apparently reported nothing of this, and poor George looked somewhat grey in the face at the latest development. I heard the sounds of commotion from beyond the room, of a struggle and harsh words and a single outcry thick with pain and anger.

I have heard the warm say that their "blood froze" when faced with the unthinkable. I don't recall ever experiencing such while I was a mortal girl, but I recognized the voice behind that scream, and for a moment it was as if my every artery had been infected with ice.

The door opened, and at first it was filled with the two large men who wrestled between them the accuser Duerr had summoned into the room. A step inside, however, and they thrust the witness forward, manacled but still restrained as well by cruel hands. Her clothing was torn and had clearly seen rough use, and was stained by blood and worse. Her lower lip was broken, and I glimpsed a gap where a tooth had been. Her hair was a tangle, her face darkened by bruise and swollen almost beyond recognition.

Almost. For the battered disguise was not enough to hide her from me. It was my own dear Red Lantern, Li-hua, brought into the house of her enemies to bring me down.

The crowd erupted in confusion, and several of the Legation Ladies were forced to fan themselves for fear of fainting upon viewing the condition of the prisoner. The latter's dark eyes were on me alone, however. I could see the fear in them still, but knew it had been tempered just enough by the sight of me in custody. In her gaze was the dark energy of superstition spiked with the fury of love lost. I silently mouthed the syllables for "I'm sorry," toward her, but given the lack of response from those pitiless eyes I might as well have not made the attempt.

As she was brought forward, my study of my would-be accuser told me more of her plight. Li-hua had been beaten, surely, and cruelly manacled. However, it was also clear by the damage to her raiment, and the way she carried herself, that she had been viciously raped; this sweet virgin girl who had before only known my kisses and, once, just once, the gentle invasion of my fingers. I knew I could expect no quarter from such a witness, and yet the fury I found building within me was not for her but for my fellow Legation dwellers, who could see her so used and then cavalierly brought in to bear witness without even the courtesy of a rag to wash herself with before testifying.

Miho slipped from the room, as if she sensed the explosion building in my little form and was fearful of being drawn into the blast when it came. George, battered by the earlier testimony, looked upon Li-hua with dismay. He was not an ignorant man, and I'm sure he sensed and was outraged by at least some of the things that had been done to her, but his questions and his concerns all centered upon what sort of accusations she might fling at me.

If Duerr was even aware of his witness's condition, his speech betrayed nothing.

"So, my Lords, what have we here?" he began. "Is it another misjudged innocent somehow discovered in Red Lantern clothing? Oh, I think not...." He turned at this and flung his voice at Li-hua, as if it were a stone that could further break her flesh. "Are you or are you not a so-called 'sister-disciple' of the Red Lanterns?"

She spit towards him, but the spittle was thick and stained with blood, and only managed to streak her chin before disappearing into the red ruin of her blouse.

"Kill all the foreign devils, and make the churches burn!" she hissed.

Duerr applauded, as if she were one of his convert children struggling through the English alphabet.

"I believe I would be forgiven if I interpreted that as a 'yes?'" He said.

"Enough!" I cried. I was on my feet, all thought of maintaining a demure presence to deflect suspicion gone. "You dare continue this sham while the very witness you present shows evidence of crimes that should make your own cold blood boil?"

The minister fairly pranced, so pleased was he at having provoked this outburst.

"'A hit,'" he quoted, "'a very palpable hit.' It seems Miss Jinyu is acquainted with the witness, else why such a violent response? Oh, the woman we are here to judge was most assuredly a Red Lantern, she *was*, but is there more? Would not even such a ragtag militia expect one of its own to be impassive in the face of harm done to a comrade? But perhaps not when the person so harmed was a lover, a sister in the sins of Sappho, perhaps?"

The poetic reference might have been little more than mumbo-jumbo to Li-hua, but clearly she had something to say, whether in reply to Duerr's taunting or no. She raised a manacled hand toward me while I met her eyes (in truth, I dared not look away for fear of what I would reveal about myself by doing so) and, her throat clearly parched and her voice further filtered through swollen lips and broken teeth, delivered her condemnation.

"She is not Red Lantern," Li-hua announced, each word clearly paining her. "False Lantern, she is a shape shifter, a demon!"

This was perhaps a surfeit of blessings for the poor minister, who might well have believed in demons in his own secret heart but surely realized the futility of trying to sell the supernatural to a group of seasoned diplomats who were, worse yet, fearing death from very natural and immediate causes at the time. He tut-tutted, looked to his audience for sympathy, and tried again.

"My Lords," he appealed, obsequious to a fault, "do we not already know that the rebels are infected with the basest superstitions? Is it a surprise, then, that this witness brings tales of the demonic to our hearing? Let us ignore these ravings and consider the facts: she clearly knows the woman who calls herself Jinyu Liu, a female who had a Red Lantern blouse secreted among her bed things. These details alone, regardless of the pagan misconceptions that have obviously overthrown the poor mind of she who testifies here, are enough, are they not, to lead to one unavoidable conclusion?

"That Jinyu Liu is a Red Lantern, sent among us to parse out our strengths and weaknesses by seducing the one man among us who has his finger upon the very pulse of our resistance. I charge you to dare to reach the only possible conclusion, and to take whatever difficult actions might be required to assure our safety in the face of this subversive invasion."

The delegates conferred among themselves as he sat down, clearly satisfied with his own rhetoric, and I prepared myself for action as Sir Claude rose to speak. The old war-horse appeared grave, and shuffled a sheaf of papers in his hands thoughtfully, placing these on the desk in front of him and aligning their pages with a few strokes of a finger before addressing the room.

"It seems," he began, "that we have no shortage of demons here. The condition of this witness provides me with ample evidence of such un-Christian activities, and that alone would invalidate her testimony in any civilized court of law."

Duerr rose to object, but MacDonald waved him down with an impatient hand.

"What has been proven here," he said, "and without the slightest doubt, is that we in this Enclave are capable of an atrocity the equal of any perpetrated by our enemies. The witness will remain in custody, and benefit from whatever medical aid we have available to us. I will personally examine her when this is done to satisfy myself that all possible measures are taken to speed her healing.

"There are, to be sure, legitimate questions concerning Miss Jinyu, but none that rise to the level of certainty. I propose that Mr. Morrison do without her aid, whatever if might have consisted of. As I recall he was quite capable of stirring the world's pot before her arrival. Rather than be taken into custody, when no crime has been proven, she will be sent to the Fu, there to dwell until the current crisis has spent itself, and where it seems she should have been housed from the moment of her arrival here."

Chapter Seventeen

If I had expected Morrison to rise one last time as my champion (which I confess I did not), I would have been disappointed. The allegations against me, and perhaps most telling the thought that I had been Li-hua's lover before I became his own, had quite unmanned him, and he sat in silence as I was led away. I briefly considered making a move to free the Red Lantern, as well, but the expression on her face convinced me that any aid from such as me would have been spurned; and so, bereft of a plan for the moment, I allowed myself to be led into the Fu, my bedroll and all within it lost to me.

Conditions there had worsened since my arrival in the Legations. As I had speculated, whatever food shortages were faced by the complex as a whole had been ameliorated by tightening the belts of these unfortunates. Rice there was, but not enough, and so it was stretched with sawdust and other indigestibles. Where the Westerners were reduced to slaughtering horses and mules for red meat, those parts that they would not consume, including the heads and offal, were provided to the Chinese Christians, and even these were fought over. Disease, including malaria, vied with starvation to tally the most fatalities. Where humankind, by virtue of their abbreviated life spans, might appear to the Kin as dogs and cats would to mortals, those in the Fu had become the mayflies of humanity

None of these hardships, of course, had any impact upon me. The illnesses that plagued the living were helpless against my physiognomy, and the very suffering to which the denizens of the Fu were subjected made this hell hole a veritable cornucopia to one of the Kin. Therefore as soon as darkness provided a shield for my activities, I restored my flagging energies with the aid of a malaria sufferer. If in doing so I hurried his inevitable death, at least I provided the doomed man with a few moments of unprecedented pleasure as I sped him along that road.

As to the numbers of Chinese then maintained in the Fu, it remained impossible to provide an accurate estimation. There were certainly some thousands, with the tally of the dying for a long time kept pace with by those arriving destitute and in many cases with terrible wounds. Where those Westerners in the Legations managed to keep a stiff upper lip, sporting formal and even tennis flannels despite the siege, the unfortunates among whom I found myself had long since abandoned any effort at grooming, as often appearing mostly unclothed or naked as dressed, and moving only when necessary to scrabble for a bit of food or to move from the patch of earth they had already soiled.

If I had needed any further proof of man's base inhumanity, or of the power of myth (both Western and

Chinese) to inflame it, I could have found evidence aplenty in those circumstances. However instructive or comfortable for me the Fu might have been, however, it was a form of prison nonetheless, and with the fate of the Delegations still uncertain, and Huo as capricious as ever, my work was unfinished. Though I had no idea how to bring it to a satisfactory conclusion, I knew that my current state could provide no progress, and so determined that I must move yet again.

When Sir Claude had relegated me to the Fu, he had reasoned that no one would dare leave its poor comforts for the dangers without (unless of course I was a Red Lantern, a conjecture that I think he had quite dismissed). Therefore he had given little thought to the possibility of my escape. The question remained, however, of where I should go once beyond the Enclave's walls.

In speaking with those of my fellow inmates who were still willing or able to talk, I learned that the Peitang Cathedral, only a few miles away, was also still under siege by the Boxers. Furthermore, I learned that its master, Bishop Favier, was viewed as a champion by many of the Chinese Christians, who considered him wiser and better prepared than the leaders of the Legations, and indulged in grudging envy for the reportedly better conditions in which their Catholic brothers and sisters were kept under his patronage.

I determined to try to reach this fortress church, both to see if my disappointment with the treatment of the denizens of the Fu might be lessened by what I found there, and because I suspected that Huo, no stranger to ego, might decide to direct her attacks toward the point where the resistance was most steadfast.

Filth is a most convenient and efficient disguise. That which repels the eye (and the nose) is not apt to suffer careful study, and fortunately the necessary cosmetics were all around me. This would prove especially effective for me, I thought, since my efforts at personal cleanliness (driven by amorous circumstance as they were rather than any obsession with sanitation) had been remarked upon several times over the course of my time in China.

So, and not without regrets given that it was the only outfit I currently owned, I managed to rend my blue shirt and trousers dramatically, and let their cuffs and hem accumulate what they would in my travels through the Fu. Blood was of course also in goodly supply all around me, drying upon the wounds of those who had been injured beyond saving. This I used to besmirch the flesh beneath the tears in my clothing, and also to slick down the hair on the right side of my skull and to paint the flesh around and beneath it to simulate a head injury.

Thus decorated as fiercely as any Red Indian brave ever was, I wandered, seemingly aimless, through the quarter and, in the same apparently dazed manner, past the Italian troops who were charged with defending a segment of the Fu's border. These men were under steady fire, the Boxers and their Imperial allies having thrown a fierce attack at the area, and, truth be told, were likely not adverse to seeing one poor soul stagger out beyond the borders, the loss meaning one less mouth to feed.

Once beyond the boundaries I was relieved to find myself unmolested. Perhaps the nominal supervision provided by the Qing's forces had managed to focus the Boxer's ire more clearly upon their known enemies rather than targets of opportunity, or it might have been simply that, in my apparent condition, I was presumed close enough to death to ignore. At any rate I managed to make my way through the chaos that surrounded me, though occasionally being forced to detour around the more frenzied mobs and step gingerly over corpses of man and beast. The Cathedral was a scant three kilometers from the Enclave, but these diversions, and the wandering progress which I affected, probably resulted in my covering twice that distance.

When seen from afar the church appeared to be almost inviolate, an imposing (if garish) structure that quite stood out in its company, like a stage beauty amongst a crowd of tradeswomen. As I approached closer, however, I could see the damage done by shot and shell to its twin spires, and the blackened and smoldering ruins of other edifices all round about, which had almost certainly suffered from Huo's attentions.

My next hurdle would be the problem of gaining entrance. The gunfire from within, though parsimonious, was accurate to the extreme, and those within the fortress church had little reason to expect friends from outside their walls. I lurked for a good while beyond the range of rifle shot, and hoped to spy an opening.

As I waited and watched my eyes happened to fall upon a small cache of rifles, strewn like jackstraws and abandoned in the no-man's-land between the Cathedral walls and the armies outside, presumably by a contingent of Imperial troops who had fled in the face of accurate opposing fire. This prize had not escaped the eyes of the defenders, and before long a small force burst free of the barricades with the clear goal of retrieving these weapons for use within.

The soldiers came under withering fire as they did so, however, and I determined that this was the time to try my luck. Shouting "friend, friend" as I ran (though the troops I approached were one and all French, I could only hope that they had this much English among them), I managed to scoop up one of the rifles and, with it in hand, joined the party as it retreated rapidly back to the relative safety of the Cathedral complex.

I stumbled as I entered the church grounds, having taken (without initially noticing) a bullet through my left calf. This was not a telling wound, of course, but its brief blood-letting only served to augment my damaged appearance. I was quickly relieved of the rifle and continued to cry out "friend" in both English and Manchu, to the apparent confusion of those around me. A soldier was sent off, however, and soon returned with a translator to aid me in explaining my presence, the gift of the abandoned firearm not enough to completely offset the suspicions of my new companions.

Still on my knees, my first sight of this individual consisted of little more than a pair of crude, heavy shoes. Before I could investigate further, I heard a gasp of surprise, and the new arrival spoke in tones of wonder.

"It's you!" she said.

Chapter Eighteen

It was of course Belle, the minister's daughter whose family I had managed to spare by disavowing their faith when confronted by Boxers on the road from Tientsin. With a brief flurry of French, which served to ease the doubts of the soldiers, she had me taken to a nearby hut in order to see to my injuries.

The small space was crowded, and thick with the stink of fever. I realized at once that I had been transported to a makeshift infirmary, occupied by a number of the wounded and disease-ridden who had already fallen victim to the siege. As Belle washed the worst of the dirt and blood from my face and hair, I managed to inform her that I was not badly injured but merely befouled as a result of my time spent in the compound of the Chinese Christians in the Legations. This news was apparently of great interest so, having determined that I could walk, she shouted again to those lingering outside the hut and led me, still limping, to an audience with those who could most benefit from my news.

Our halting progress soon took us into the Cathedral itself, and there into the company of the two men most responsible for the continued resistance within the besieged compound. The first of these proved to be none other than Bishop Favier, a stout and imposing man with a great white beard and an intelligent, martial air all at odds with his ecclesiastical hat and vestments. The second was a young man, slender and dark, with a sharp fringe of facial hair and military vestments. This, I soon learned, was Lieutenant Paul Henry, the 23-year-old Breton who, along with a detachment of thirty French sailors, had been sent to Peitang by the Delegation's French Minster, M. Pichon, at the Bishop's request, and upon whose young shoulders the defense of the Cathedral had ultimately fallen.

Belle spoke to these worthies briefly, apparently telling them that I had until late been resident in the Legation complex, a revelation that brought forth a flurry of questions in French. My translator was quite overwhelmed by this, and was forced to ask the pair to repeat their inquiries several times, and in a more relaxed cadence, before she was able to gather the gist of their concerns, which seemed to involve my telling them anything and everything I could about the situation I had left, the residents of the Cathedral having had no word from the Legations despite their proximity and long fearing the worst.

I provided what information I could, assuring them that the Enclave still stood and appeared to be in no imminent danger of capture. I told them as well of the sometimes contradictory communications those in that compound had received from the Qing, of the death of von Ketteler, and of the threatening shortages of food and ammunition. Though I would have called my news dire, the pair seemed to take heart from it, and instructed Belle to find me a place to rest and give me with what comfort she could.

With my assurances that I was not on the verge of expiring and more in need of bathing than bandages, Belle found me quarters in another room that was equally crowded but not with those in such desperate straits as in the hut to which she had previously taken me. There she provided me with cloths and water and as I completed the cleaning she had begun, preserving what little modesty I could in the process, we described to each other the events that had transpired since our parting (my narrative, to be sure, incorporating editing as the circumstances required).

Belle and her family had made for Pekin after being dismissed by my red-clad captives, trusting in the Imperial army to keep the bloodthirsty insurgents away from the capitol itself. In this they were sorely disappointed, of course. Soon after entering the city they were spotted by a small band of Boxers. Her father had, to hear her tell it, fought an heroic rear guard, armed only with his staff against the swords and pikes of his enemies, and had fallen in their defense, buying his family time enough to escape into the Cathedral.

Knowing the animosity that existed between Catholic and Protestant, Belle's mother had resisted this decision, and the girl had been forced to drag her and the infant by main force into the church grounds, where to their great relief they were accepted with open arms. It seems that Favier, wiser than many of his compatriots, recognized that all Christians were one in the eyes of the enemy, and thus must be the same in the eyes of their God were any to survive.

Belle had taken guidance from this interdenominational liberalism and soon turned to lending her hand wherever she might. Her French at the time was limited to the rudiments she had picked up during her education at home, but it quickly flowered, as the grasp of a foreign language will when it is the only tongue spoken around one. Thus she became a de facto translator, as well as a sort of nurse-of-all-trades, attending to the wounded and sick; the latter of which were many, as the deplorable conditions within bred a slew of diseases, including an outbreak of small pox, that were only controlled by the most heroic efforts.

In this way she had come to be recognized as an asset to the community, and (as I had just witnessed) was even at times consulted by Bishop Favier and Lieutenant Henry on linguistic matters. I learned as well, from the tone of her discussion and a fine blush that crept upon her fair cheeks when discussing him, that she had grown quite enamored with the young Breton, though remained in doubt as to whether her affections were reciprocated.

Thus when Belle learned, in the course of my own narrative, that I had been present at the battles around Tientsin, nothing would do but that I be brought before the two leaders again and provide them with what insights I could regarding the prospects in that city.

This I did, giving them essentially the same summary I had provided Morrison, augmented by the information that he had received from his messenger, Jie. Favier in particular seemed heartened by this information, having placed less hope in Seymour's relief expedition than had those in the

Legation. He informed me that food and ammunition were their chief concerns, as they had been in the Enclave, but that active rationing from the first (which I had seen evidence of in the sporadic, if accurate, gunfire from within the compound) assured him that they would be able to resist for some time to come.

I did not, of course, dwell upon my career as a Red Lantern, other than to confess that I had so disguised myself to avoid murder, and made no mention of my time as a guest in Cixi's dungeon. I avoided, as well, any mention of Huo, fearing that any hint of the supernatural might inflame my hosts against me. I was soon to learn, though, that the creature herself had no such qualms about making her presence known.

With this second audience concluded, during which I could not help but notice that young Henry cast an admiring glance or two at my companion, Belle returned me to my quarters and offered me what passed for dinner in those times. I again pled exhaustion, and found once more that want on the part of my companion allowed her to easily ignore my lack of appetite.

It being midday, I did not have to feign a need for sleep, and despite the brutal temperatures outside, which rendered the interior of even the hut quite oven-like and served to exaggerate the scent of the unwashed individuals with whom I shared its space, I allowed myself to slip into the death-like torpor that passes for rest among the Kin. Nightfall came all too soon, and with it Belle, who seemed to shake off fatigue in the tradition of angels of mercy throughout song and story, arrived to invite me to assist her in her evening rounds.

DRAGON BLOOD

Medicines were among the many things that the far-sighted Favier had labored to stockpile when the specter of the Boxers had first risen in the countryside, though at the time the most experienced of Western "China hands" had given little thought to the uprising. Most of these items, I found, were being used to treat the ill and those refugees who had arrived at the Cathedral already damaged, as there were remarkably few wounded among the small garrison protecting the complex despite the regular fusillade of rifle and cannon fire to which they were subjected. Disease and starvation, the latter particularly among the very young, were the principle enemies here it seemed.

Belle tended to one and all, reckless of her own health in the face of contagion, and secreting away morsels from her own inadequate meals to force upon those in the direst need. I helped her as I could, though providing comfort had never been my forte, and in her single-minded dedication I found as much to admire as I had found actions to be despised among most of humanity. It was perhaps this, and my amusement concerning her so-far unrequited affection for Henry (and certainly not any lingering loyalty to Morrison, or so I assured myself), that convinced me to resist any amorous inclinations I might have had toward her, though she was certainly appealing and, as the reader by now surely knows, my romantic tastes are decidedly, how shall I put this, catholic?

So for a time I worked chastely at her side, the unlikeliest of Florence Nightingale's heirs. Though I could have occasionally used the talents of the Kin to heal more effectively than I did, I had learned my lesson at Morrison's bedside and resisted the urge to do so, relying instead on the appearance of care and the rude medicines provided by Belle. All the while, however, my thoughts turned regularly to Huo, to what card the creature might play next, and to what I might have in my poor hand to counter her.

I received my first hint on June 28th, when those of us within the Cathedral community looked out, perplexed, as a group of Boxers rolled a pair of the water pumps normally used in firefighting up close to our main entry. Shielding themselves as well as possible behind these ungainly devices, the warriors put their shoulders to the pump and a stream of liquid shot forth. The biting stink of it soon told us that it was not water but petrol that was being sprayed against the gate.

A Boxer with a torch quickly turned the pumper into a flame thrower, and while both troops and civilians within the complex were frantically working to douse these fires, and accurate rifle work drove the arsonists away from their machines (several of them in flames themselves as a result of the hazards of these crude weapons), I caught a glimpse of a flash of red in the air.

It was Huo, of course, and seemingly with a wave of her fans (which I'm sure were pure theater and not necessary to the creature's fire-starting capabilities), she had ignited a blaze upon the Cathedral roof itself. Only the most desperate efforts served to douse these flames, and I'm sure I heard the creature's laughter as she drifted off into the sky to ply her terrible trade elsewhere.

None but me, it seems, had perceived the abomination (or at least admitted having done so), and as soon as the fires were out talk within the Cathedral turned to destroying the houses from which the water-pump attack was launched. A small force set out to do this, and fighting fire with fire (under careful cover from riflemen within the barricades) was able to burn the dwellings and capture the two pumps which the Boxers had deployed against us. These proved too dangerous and unreliable for use within the confined quarters of the Cathedral, and thus were never employed defensively, but at least with their confiscation the enemy was deprived of their use as well.

I was convinced, however, that these infernal machines had only been intended as a distraction, and that the chief danger to the survival of the Cathedral, and the besieged Legations as well, lay with other plans being developed by Huo. In the immediate days ahead, though, we were faced with nothing but the more predictable attacks from Imperial cannon and rifle fire, which, as was the case in both Tientsin and the Pekin Enclaves, produced far more sound and fury than actual damage.

Thus the Cathedral complex did not suffer too many casualties from military activity, despite the constant bombardment, and hunger and illness remained the primary specters that haunted those under siege. On July 11th, however, we became aware of a new threat, which was to prove the most deadly developed by our enemies yet, and once again Huo played a part in it.

Lieutenant Henry and others had warned the Bishop for some time of observations that hinted that the Boxers might be attempting to tunnel under the Cathedral complex, presumably to open up avenues by which to invade. He had even set work forces consisting of Chinese Christians to do their own digging in an attempt to intercept such earthworks, but to no avail. On the 11th, however, the real reason for this activity was revealed, when an explosive charge set beneath the northeast corner of the complex was detonated. The resulting blast fortunately resulted in only one fatality, but its implications were dire. Setting off such a charge far underground would have been hazardous at best for those tasked with doing so, and I was certain to me that Huo's incendiary talents had enabled it to be done without risk.

The second blast, which was the result of explosives placed beneath the compound to the west of the initial attack, was far more serious. Those still asleep were shaken from their beds early on the 18th, and as would-be rescuers rushed to the site they came upon a scene of terrible destruction, with a great crater surrounded by corpses, and the torn pieces of other victims, still smoking in the quiet morning air. When the would-be rescuers, who braved heavy rifle fire to bring out the dead and wounded, had completed their grisly work the mortalities stood at 28, making this by far the single deadliest action in the siege to date.

It was a poor omen for a day that had yet to expend its allotment of tragic news, as I was to discover hours later. After weeks of silence, a messenger had managed to reach Peitang from the Legations. It seems the Chinese troops had continued their assault on the Fu, and on the 16th Captain Strouts, commander of the British contingent, and George Morrison had been returning from delivering a relief force to that conflict and had come under fire. Strouts was killed and George wounded, though how gravely the message bearer was unable to say.

Chapter Nineteen

I learned of Morrison's injury thanks to the courtesy of Bishop Favier, and the translation provided by dear Belle. There was other news included in the report, as well, but I confess I heard nothing, or at least accorded little else any attention, after this revelation.

The minister's daughter noted my reaction, and questioned me about it as we left the priest's quarters.

"This monsieur Morrison, he is a friend of yours," she asked, still caught up between French and English.

I considered how to answer, but found that I had not the heart for subterfuge, so replied simply and truthfully.

"We were...we were intimate," I said.

Belle's eyes grew wide.

"An Australian journalist and a Chinese girl?" she marveled, "Surely that created a scandal among the Legations?"

"Hence my presence here," I said, it being easier to agree to her simple analysis than to detail the story of my inquisition, and perhaps safer to do so, as well.

My companion was silent for a moment, but when she replied it was with a stubborn confidence.

"If you love him you must go to him," she said.

I sighed. It seemed impossible to explain to this girl, particularly when she was herself caught up in the tangle of romanticism, the complexity of my feelings. On the one hand my relationship with Morrison was little more than a reflection of my own greed for pleasure, and yet that hunger would not have been ignited had I not been moved by admiration for the man. To go beyond that and explain my dalliance with Li-hua and George's apparent denial of me would be another step altogether too far. In the end I equivocated.

"I cared for him," I said, "but I believe it is over." Then, in order to change the topic of conversation, I asked a question that had been nagging at me since the meeting with Favier earlier that day.

"Your French improves my leaps and bounds, Belle, have you discovered an aptitude for languages?"

It was her turn to go briefly silent, and it was as if I could see the thoughts shuffle and undergo consideration beneath her long brown hair; which I suddenly noticed was, if not styled, at least clean and carefully brushed to better frame her pale face and large walnut-colored eyes.

"I am studying," she finally allowed. "The war will not last forever, and I will need some sort of a career if I am to be more than just another maiden dreaming of being a wife."

We had continued to walk while we spoke, and I saw that we were nearing the small house in which she and several other women, all the daughters or widows of men of the cloth, were garrisoned together.

"Being a wife is thought to be the ultimate aim for young womanhood in much of the world today," I said. She hurried to interject before I could go on.

"Oh, I hope to be married," she said, "but I think a woman who can assist the family by doing something other than bear and care for children, a wife who has her own occupation and can thus add to the family coffer, might not only be more likely to find a husband but be better able to keep him."

I was surprised, and I confess charmed, by this unexpected air of Modernity, and was about to comment upon it when we were interrupted.

"Miss Belle, ready start lesson now?"

I turned toward the voice's clear, if heavily accented, English, and was not at all surprised to find myself facing a smiling Lieutenant Henry.

"So you are learning English, monsieur?" I asked, favoring him with a little curtsey that did not at all befit my second-hand rags.

Belle rushed in to answer.

"I am helping the Lieutenant with my language," she said, "and in return he is working with me to expand my abilities with his own."

By the Frenchman's smile and nod I knew that he had understood the gist of this, and, despite my own concerns, I could not subdue a small grin of my own.

Belle clearly noted my reaction, and now it was her turn to divert the conversation back toward the direction it had formerly taken and thus redirect attention to me.

"Jinyu Liu has just learned that her lover has been shot in an attack on the Legations," she said,

"Mon Dieu!" replied Henry, drawing himself up to befit the dramatic nature of this revelation, before continuing in English, glancing at Belle as he did to judge her reaction to his attempt. "My God! Does he live? It is hard for the Chinese there, I believe?"

Again the girl interjected before I was able.

"The gentleman is Australian," she said, "a famous journalist."

If M. Henry was shocked by this, he had the wherewithal to hide any signs of such prejudice, and continued as if this were not a scandalous revelation.

"But the *gentilhomme*," he continued manfully, "does he live?"

I managed to speak before Belle, fearing that if I did not my companions might carry on the entire conversation without me.

"I do not know the nature of his injury, monsieur, only that he has been shot.

"Then you must go!" said the Lieutenant, before slipping into his own language in a rush of feeling, "*Il n'y a qu'un bonheur dans la vie, c'est d'aimer et d'être aimé.*"

This required Belle to purse her lips as she worked through the translation.

"Henry says," she began, with a fond glance at the Frenchman, "that love is the only happiness in life. That is very beautiful, don't you think?"

"It would be difficult to go," I replied, skirting the question and Belle's obvious preoccupation with matters romantic. "To this day only one messenger has gotten through, and I do not know how I would be welcomed, by Mr. Morrison or the Delegation at large."

Henry's expression grew brave and tragic.

"If I had fifty men not thirty," he said gallantly, "I would free the city to make clear your way."

Despite my worries I could not help but be charmed by this chivalry.

"Would that all men shared your sensibility, good Henry," I replied. "But Belle perhaps overstates the case. The gentleman and I have been intimate, yes, but I fear that love was never mentioned between us."

The poor Frenchman! I fear that this concept was quite beyond his understanding, and that he would as soon engage in loveless pleasure as he would disobey an order. Finding the very idea of what I had described impossible, he of course choose to ignore it.

"You must go," he repeated, made bullheaded by his own finer feelings. "Only a brute would spurn you when faced with such evidence of your concern!"

"And you shall!" Belle broke in. "Henry must stay here, his duty demands it, but I will accompany you!"

"If I go, dear heart," I replied, a stern glance punctuating my words, "and I have by no means decided to do so, you certainly will not accompany me. A Western woman would not survive long on the streets of Pekin, and with you gone how would the good Lieutenant continue his studies?"

She was abashed by this, but I think saw her own rashness, and in that realization was able to listen to the whispering of her own heart. I, however, was in a quandary. Should I indeed be able to accomplish what only I and one messenger had before (and I was smug enough to believe that I could, given the advantages I had over any mortal note-bearer), I could perhaps re-enter the Fu without my absence having been noted. But how might I contact Morrison without risking discovery by one of those who had earlier judged me; and more telling still, what would I do if I managed to obtain that access only to have any communications denied?

While I so contemplated the options my two companions eyed me, waiting a reply, and occasionally sneaking surreptitious glances at each other. They of course knew nothing of Huo, or of my growing suspicion that in the tunnel bombs the creature had come up with a means of breaking the siege of the Cathedral, and had perhaps even been so directed by Cixi in hopes that in sacrificing this stronghold she might spare the Delegations and thus her Empire. Or of my belief that Huo was not under the Dowager's control at all, and might bring down the Qing despite her. It was as if their world was scripted by a love-struck sonneteer, while mine was better aligned with the works of Machiavelli.

Yet it was difficult, afloat as I was in a sea of hatred, with the blame so evenly distributed between West and East, to not clutch hold of and cling to the lifebuoy of their jejune innocence. Truth be told I had no other plan, and to remain as I was would likely resign me to the role of spectator to events that would unravel as Huo wished. Perhaps action, even if it was aimless and likely futile, would at least trigger a response that I could reply to in kind. So I rolled my eyes, wrung loose a long sigh and surrendered.

"You've convinced me," I said, taking one of each of their hands in mine, "I will go."

Chapter Twenty

I quickly determined that it would be best to attempt to reach the Legations under cover of darkness. Not only would many potentially spying eyes be closed in sleep, but the new clothing that Belle had provided me (which was of the same hue as my original peasant garb) would provide a form of camouflage, and the stealth of Kindred movement would render me all but invisible. I was hopeful that these advantages would allow me to traverse the short distance between the Cathedral and my objective undetected.

Both Henry and Belle were eager to offer advice, and I listened politely though many of their suggestions were more applicable to a mortal than to a so-called "Creature of the Night." I recognized their need to feel helpful, however, and gave the appearance of considering their input carefully, regardless of my intentions to largely ignore it.

There was, however, one boon I could ask of my friend. Unrolling my sash and retrieving the wire recording spools hidden therein, I begged of Belle the pad and pencil she always carried to aid in her translation work. With these I scrawled out a London address I had reason to know by heart, and pressed this and the cylinders upon her.

"When the siege is broken and post is once more possible," I said with an air of optimism I little felt, "please see that these are sent off. I fear their discovery or loss in the adventure ahead of me." This the girl readily agreed to do, noting that it was a small enough parting favor.

Henry was also insistent that I accept a farewell gift, which he presented to me while insisting that it was to be considered an offering from them both. The device he offered to me was a hand torch fired by an internal generator that was charged by repeatedly squeezing a lever on its shaft. It was clear to me that this had been a gift from some well-meaning family member upon his departure for the Middle Kingdom, as the machine was far too ornate (the lever was decorated with brass drollery, for example) to be an item of military issue. I accepted this gratefully, and tucked it into my sash.

Simply leaving the compound provided a challenge. Those guarding the complex had been astute enough when I arrived, but in the wake of Huo's tunnel attacks one and all were quite on edge, and I was concerned that, should I be observed leaving the area, I might become a target for rifle fire. A bullet to the body would, of course, be only a temporary convenience, but even the Kin can be vulnerable to a shot to the brain or one that severs the spine.

Here Henry was able to proffer one final parting favor. When we had said our goodbyes (mine filled with premonition, as it seemed to me that my Chinese adventure was, one way or another, drawing to a close), the Lieutenant strolled to a separate section of the barricades and there, in a voice full of urgency, called for help in anticipating an imaginary threat. The pickets surrounding me rushed to the aid of their revered commander, and I slipped out and into the Pekin night.

The evening was overcast, with clouds that had of late frequently arrived to swell and gather with the belated return of the rains. There was not a breath of wind, and the heat of the day lingered, generating a torrid humidity that draped itself over the city like a damp sheet, causing the night noises to seem to come from every direction at once, and exaggerating the smells of the cooking pots and corpses that surrounded me.

Despite the latter, however, the darkness was a boon, and I was able to move quickly. Thus the sudden loom of the Legations appeared surprisingly soon. The Fu, I found, was still serving as the focus for enemy action, and was ringed with the red-yellow of guttering fires, those of the Boxers close to the walls and as randomly distributed as a toss of coins, while the cook pits of the Imperial army were set further back and arrayed in neat regimental order.

I paused at the edge of this living minefield, and mentally plotted my course. I have learned that human nature predisposes one to become alert at the first notice of an unidentified sound in the darkness, to then remain alert to see if the disturbance is repeated, and only after the second such mystery actually rise to investigate the cause. Thus I determined that, once my route was selected, I would proceed quickly and without hesitation, in order to lessen the chance that a second misstep would occur too near to the site of the first.

This strategy served me well, and though I triggered curious grumbling on those occasions when I ventured too close to my sleeping (or nearly so) enemies, no alarm was raised by my passing. Thus I soon found myself at the very walls of my objective and, waiting there until a pair of guards were briefly distracted by conversation, found myself without incident back among the concentrated suffering that was the Fu.

Here I paused. Those who have never been in the presence of mass starvation might wonder at my claim that it has a stink of its own; but there is a bitter acridity produced as the body consumes itself in desperation, and this stench had grown far stronger during my absence. It was clear to me that, should the siege go on too much longer, the Fu would become more mass grave than refuge.

There were guards stationed between the quarter occupied by the starving Chinese Christians and the Western segment of the Legations, though I doubted whether the denizens of the former were capable of any concerted action that would threaten the marginally superior resources of the latter. These pickets seemed to offer my best chance of communicating my desire to speak to Morrison, but I found that their ears were deaf to my entreaties, closed by necessity against an endless chorus of cries for food or aid.

The torch that Henry had gifted me with was little more than an expensive toy, but rarity exaggerates value, and there was certainly not another like it among the thousands of sufferers in the Fu. Thus when I squeezed its generator lever and shined the light upon one of the guards, it brought the response that the most fervent of my pleas had failed to produce.

"You, woman, what have you got there?" he called out in English, shielding his eyes against the brightness with one hand.

I stepped closer and turned the light away from his face, pumping the lever to increase its shine.

"It is a hand torch," I said, "possibly useful to one burdened with the night watch? It is yours if you will convey a message for me to George Morrison."

He held out his hand, but I whipped mine behind my back, hiding the prize.

"When the message has been conveyed and a reply brought to me it will be yours," I said.

It must have occurred to the guard that he could simply take the torch from me, it being usually easiest to steal from those who have the least, but he seemed a good-hearted man despite his cruel duty, and after a moment's thought he replied.

"Give me your message and be quick about it," he said. "I go off duty as soon as my relief arrives, and a cup of tea, even if it is only the stuff that passes for it here, will be waiting for me, and even your pretty toy will not keep me from it for long."

"My name is Jinyu Liu," I said. 'Tell him where I am. Tell him that I must speak to him."

"That gentleman took a bullet in the buttocks," he replied, "or so they says anyways, so I'm not sure how keen he'll be for a midnight rendezvous, but that's not on me. I'll give him your message straightaway. Be sure you're here when I return."

Moments later the tromp of boots announced the arrival of a new shift to the Fu border post, and after a quick whispered conference, probably more concerned with the gossip of the evening than any news generated by his thankless duty, my messenger hurried off. I sat in the dirt to wait, letting hope and dread duel in my imagination while the minutes crept slowly by.

He was not long I think in returning, but those who have waited will know that time is far more variable in nature than the simple gears of a clock can comprehend.

When the guard arrived and I saw his face, I almost bid him not speak, so clearly was the news etched upon his weary features. Some men become only harder when faced with a cruel situation, while others find a new sensitivity that strengthens as matters deteriorate. He was one of the latter, it seems, and reluctant to be the deliverer of another's pain.

I did not, however, hold up a hand to forestall him, or beg him to leave his message unspoken. Instead I sat and waited, as compliant as one who has given up on holding back the executioner's axe and only wishes it hurried toward its end.

"Mr. Morrison recovers nicely from his pusillanimous wound," he said, generous answering a question I had not asked and gently seeking to devaluate the message sender as he did so. "He wishes you well, but asks you to understand that any further communication would little profit either of you." The guard paused, watching the brickbats of his words strike me most cruelly. "I'm sorry," he said.

I cannot say just what I felt. Fury, certainly, that a mere human would dare dismiss such as me, but this was tempered by the knowledge that George knew not even my race let alone my secret nature. Shame, of course, to be seen so on the ground and begging for the scraps of a man's attention. Perhaps most of all sorrow, that yet another attempt to cling to my departing humanity had left me with nothing but rope burns on my fingers.

But I stood, grateful at least that the poor light obscured the pink tint of my tears, and silently passed the torch to the messenger.

"Is there aught more I can do, miss?" he asked gently. "I feel that I've given you poor worth for your payment?"

At least I did not blubber. I managed to find control for my voice and addressed him with a calm that I did not feel. I was quite without compass, and could think of only one who might provide me with direction.

"It would be a kindness if you deliver a second message to Wakahisa Miho in the Japanese Legation and ask her to attend me here." I said.

He nodded, poor man, with the tea no doubt going cold in his barrack, and hurried off again.

Upon return, this time in seeming short order, he looked if possible more crestfallen than before.

"I fear there is no good news in me tonight, miss," he said. "That lady has vanished, and none knows where."

It was a terrible blow. I had not admitted to myself just how much I relied upon the sister-Kin woman as a lifeline, and without access to her calm guidance I found myself quite rudderless. As a result I did not stay to further taste of the guard's regret, but turned and wandered off among the dead and those soon to join them, the guard's nervous squeezing of the torch lever in my ears, a nibbling ratchet sound that grew smaller with each step.

The misery of the Fu provided no balm for mine, though I must have wandered there for some hours. Eventually I found myself, through reckless disregard alone, outside its borders again, with the morning's sun hot on my uncovered head. Strangely enough I was not soon challenged, though my blind progress took me near Boxer and Qing troops alike. It was only when I drew close to the Forbidden City that I was noticed, and soon found myself confronted by a pair of heavily armed soldiers in the company of a bald and baby-faced grandee.

"You are the woman Jinyu Liu, are you not?" asked the latter, the child's voice coming from his large frame instantly marking him as eunuch.

I only nodded, not trusting myself to speak.

"The Dowager Empress will see you," he replied.

I shook my head in the negative and turned to leave, only to find my way blocked by crossed swords.

"She *will* see you," the grandee said, and with nothing to gain or lose, I allowed myself to be led away.

Chapter Twenty-One

The corridors I was taken through showed the marks of Boxer sacrilege. Here a delicate jade figure missing the fingers most easily plucked away; there a scattering of fruit trodden into the floor whose bowl some vandal had coveted. This entropy matched my mood all too closely, and I dwelled on it as a child's tongue will worry at a loose tooth despite, or perhaps because of, the pain so caused.

When I finally came upon Cixi, the eunuch and guards leaving me at the final portal, she looked much as she had during our earlier meeting. The Empress was dressed in Imperial yellow, and again seated behind a table of sorts (perhaps the same at which I had first seen her), with a scepter beside her. I performed my kowtow, and she bade me approach.

On closer examination the Old Buddha was more clearly showing the ravages of her sixty-five years. Despite her best efforts at cosmetology, Cixi looked old and drawn, as if recent events had bent her strong backbone and banked the fires in her black eyes. She looked up at me, and for a moment seemed unsure of my identification. She fingered the staff beside her, frustration crawling over her strong, plain face, and then seemed to have worried through her hesitation.

"Ah," she said, "it is the creature who calls herself Jinyu Liu. Tell me, how do you like my dungeon?"

I considered answering falsely, but something (call it lingering sense of self-preservation) told me that such a course of action would be foolish in the extreme.

"I have been some days from your prison, Empress," I said. "The Red Lantern Li-hua released me, certainly with your concurrence?"

The dark eyes flashed at me, and in a moment the Dowager's posture became once again erect and commanding.

"So," she said, "I see at least that you are not enough of a fool to take me for one, though I confess I had thought you freed by your sponsor Huo."

"The creature is no ally of mine," I replied. "She has tolerated rather than championed me, and I think will do even that no longer. Since I was last in your illustrious presence I have only seen her from a distance, dancing in the skies."

Cixi absorbed this news in silence, drumming her fingers upon the table, those in the ornate nail protectors producing twin raps within each softer drum roll of lacquer.

"You do not belong here, Jinyu Liu," she eventually said, "and you have the look about you of one who will soon die.

Perhaps, then, my instincts were correct, and it will be safe for me to speak plainly to you."

I did not know how to respond to this pronouncement, but my pride was pricked, and I made an effort to draw myself up from despair as the Dowager herself had done.

"I do not pretend to know the future, Empress," I said, "but I hardly think my own end is imminent."

Cixi laughed at this, a knowing laugh, bitter and wry.

"None do, I've found, my pretty imposter. Even the concubine Pearl believed in her immortality until the very moment I had my eunuchs throw her down a well!"

I did not know enough about palace intrigues to parse out the meaning of this strange statement, but I could see well enough the threat hidden within it. I chose to ignore the barb altogether and to turn the conversation in a direction that would perhaps be more profitable.

"What do you seek of me, Empress? Surely you had me hunted down and brought before you for a reason?"

She paused again, eying me critically, and though she was clearly mortal I felt pinned by the sharpness of her gaze.

"I wish to unburden myself," she began, "and I wondered whether you might be an appropriate confessor. Now that I've learned that you are no longer under the protection of the thing Huo, I see that my instincts were sound. Whatever you are, creature, and please understand that I know quite well that you are no simple peasant woman named Jinyu Liu, you are no more a match for that entity than am I. Thus if I pour my soul into a vessel that is soon to be shattered, I may find the relief I require without risk that my revelations will survive to taint my memory."

Again I attempted a brave front, though the Dowager's certainty of my imminent demise only added to the black mood that was rapidly overtaking me.

"As I have not underestimated you, Empress, I would ask you to extend the same courtesy to me," I said.

"I acknowledge your gallantry, then," she replied with a thin smile, "and if I believe it is little more than a paper dragon I shall keep such musings to myself."

I did not reply to this (indeed what could I say without the risk of incurring her anger?), and the Dowager continued.

"I have been reckless," she said. "I believed, with Huo's council, that the Boxers, my people's army, could aid my forces in fighting the Western barbarians to a draw and convince them to sue for peace, guaranteeing the survival of the Qing. Now I learn that the siege of Tientsin has failed, and the corpse of that city is in the hands of my enemies.

"Huo, however, despite the promises that poured from her mouth, serves neither the Empire nor the Nation, but only her own gratification. So while the West will soon march to relieve their compatriots in Pekin. Before they do so the creature will continue to bring down first the Peitang Cathedral and then the Legations and thus glut her pleasure. Only if the Delegates survive, which I believe they cannot, is there hope for the Qing, for their death will bring a war that can only end with China in pieces.

"Thus I must leave my home here, or surely die at the hands of the barbarians as they pursue the destruction of the Forbidden City. The preparations are already underway. When my country falls I shall be far away, and hope that the interior of China is large enough, and that there are remnants enough of love for the Qing there still, to allow me to live out my remaining days in peaceful exile."

"You must not!" I interrupted, shocked into a rudeness that might in other times have cost me my head. "There is hope yet..."

Cixi regarded me with the pity the wise reserve for those who cannot see what should seem obvious.

"Hope?" she asked, her voice grown soft. "Hope is as fragile as a Boxer's invulnerability. Oh, I shall go through the motions. I will designate a Mandarin as my representative here, and bestow upon him the power to negotiate on behalf of the Empire, but I know this to be a hollow gesture. I am Empress now in name only, you see. It is Huo that rules China today, and who will spend its resources to the last man, like a child who plays at war until distracted by a new game."

"Then I will stop the creature," I said, in a show of bravado that I no longer felt. "For I am pledged that the Empire not fall. My duty demands that this be so."

Cixi clapped her hands at this demonstration, the nail-covers clicking like scorpions at play.

"As I have said, you are steadfast, miss (if even your womanhood is not a disguise). Had I an army of your like perhaps I would not find myself in these straits. But you are only one, and even now I cannot tell whether you speak the truth or dissemble to serve purposes unspoken. Go then and contest with Huo if you will, and I will travel easier knowing that my secrets will spill with your blood."

I made as if to speak again, but she stopped me with a raised hand.

"Go," she repeated. "You have witnessed history here, may that knowledge provide you with some satisfaction at the end. The Empire of the Qing has persisted for almost 300 years. Today, in your presence, it is finished."

With this Cixi rose, and rapped her scepter once upon the marble of the floor. The door opened, and admitted the eunuch and two guards to show me out. I glanced back once over my shoulder as the portal swung closed, and saw the Dowager Empress in her yellow robes, as limp as a sack full of bones, slumped upon her chair. It was the last time I was to view this remarkable woman, and her surrender weighted my steps as I was led beyond the Forbidden City and out onto the streets of Pekin, alone and burdened with knowledge that I did not know if I could bear.

Chapter Twenty-Two

My escorts had been silent and preoccupied as they led me out. I wondered, without really caring, if they had been listening at the door (a common practice among courtiers of all nations I believe), or if the news of the Dowager Empress's retreat and apparent abdication was already well known among the residents of the Forbidden City.

There was no such reticence among the crowds without, however. Another attack on the Delegations was underway, and the sounds of rifle and cannon fire were celebrated by those in the streets as a group of urchins in my own land will cheer the fireworks at a Fourth of July picnic. It seemed that at least three out of every four citizens wore red in some manner, and had I felt at all myself I might have worried for my safety in my worn peasant clothing. I had only dread for the encounter ahead, however, and did not believe that my fate rested in the hands of either Boxer or Lantern,

I was surprised, then, to find myself seized by a group of the former, who demanded, all at once, in the high-pitched voices that mark the edge of frenzy, to know my destination and allegiance. They treated me roughly, pulling first one arm and then another as if I were a wishbone, and screaming their questions willy-nilly on the heels of one another so that I could not have attempted to answer the first before the second was thrown at me.

My mind seemed numbed, and I shrugged against their capture weakly, attempting to appeal to reason. Even the knowledge that I had come from meeting with the Empress did little to calm them, if they indeed heard it above one another's shouts. It seemed as if the scene might play on indefinitely with no resolution, until I saw another Boxer rushing toward our group with his sword already drawn.

How quickly can sorrow turn on itself and generate a fierce, self-pitying anger! Suddenly I was beyond subterfuge and careless of my disguise. I felt my teeth extending of their own volition, and the red clothing of my assailants faded into a general crimson haze that colored my vision with fury.

None were dead when I walked away from the group, though given their options for medical care I will not speculate as to how many ultimately survived. The sword wielder fell last, the blade of his weapon bent over his skull, and I found myself suddenly and pointedly uninteresting to all in my immediate vicinity.

There were buildings still burning, and I scanned the skies above them for sight of Huo with no satisfaction. I screamed her name, as well, as if I could call the creature to me like a dog. Wandering, thus I searched for my enemy fruitlessly, until eventually I found myself through the gates of the city and in the countryside beyond it.

It was an eventuality I had not imagined; that I would be unable to even locate the creature and be doomed to serve as little more than an audience for her triumph. This was not to be born, and I racked my poor brain trying to discover how I might bring Huo to me for a final accounting.

The answer, when it eventually came to me (for as I have said my thoughts were awkward things, tumbling like an avalanche without order or purpose) was simplicity itself. The key had been revealed in my momentary lack of control when accosted by the Boxers within the city. Huo's tolerance had, from our first meeting, stemmed from what she called my good behavior. To draw her attention, I reasoned, I had only to abandon all subterfuge and allow myself to be what I was.

The countryside beyond Pekin was thick with people; refugees from Tientsin fleeing toward the capital from the victorious barbarians there, would-be Boxers eager to be present at the kill that all assumed was imminent, and nominal innocents abandoning that very city in fear that the mob would turn upon them in its frenzy. It offered, I determined, an appropriate stage upon which to display my talents.

I could do nothing about the color of my eyes, skin, and hair, but I was determined to be Paulette Monot again to the extent that I was able. The delicate flesh at the corners of my eyes tore as I ripped at the fine wire between them, ultimately breaking it. Though I had suffered much in my journey, that little pain was as comforting as a small pet held close, and I smiled, but it was not a pretty thing. The brief bleeding from those little wounds trailed a crimson tear beside each of my orbs, now restored to something akin to roundness, at least in my imagination. I decided the effect was appropriate.

My teeth I unsheathed as well, to the point that they extended over my lower lips even with my mouth closed. This transformation was enough to send those closest to me scattering with cries of fear. The disturbance caught the attention of a spear-wielding would-be Boxer nearby who, his sight of me blocked by the rush of bodies fleeing my company, charged forward in eager anticipation.

"Is it a foreign devil? Let me see and I will deal with it!" he cried, spear lowered as he rushed forward like a knight with a lance. The crowd melted from him as it had from me, and soon enough he was able to see the enemy he sought.

He stopped in his tracks, but did not flee, such was the courage he was able to draw from the weapon in his hands even when faced with a nightmare.

"If it is a demon you seek," I lisped around the impediment of my teeth, "you have found one. Come to me!"

I can only surmise that he believed himself in some opera fantasy, for he ran at me screaming, red-tasseled spear foremost, so fine is the line between bravery and stupidity.

It was child's play to sidestep his plunge, and as simple to break the spear with the flat of my hand and fling its parts away. The speed of my actions seemed to transfix him, and he stood there, unarmed, as petrified as any bird caught in the eyes of a serpent.

I realized that it had been some time since I'd fully fed, and with that thought the hunger that I'd been previously unaware of raged up and demanded that I tear at him. Feed I would, and at some level realized that I would needs do so before my futile contest with Huo, but I had another objective here, and it demanded that a statement be made.

My poor Boxer soon broke free of his hypnotism and attempted to flee. Before he could take three steps I was in front of him again. We repeated this dance for several more turns, cat and mouse, while the terror built within him until he reeked of it.

I took his eyes first. It was as easy as picking berries, and if he lived I wanted to leave him to a future of begging on the streets, ridiculed by children who would call his memories lies. He screamed when I did it, an animal sound that must have torn his throat. I folded him in my arms as if to offer comfort, his desperate struggles helpless beneath my strength, and buried my face in his neck.

No one was near enough to watch this embrace or to see his face relax from terror into ecstasy, and when I had swallowed enough of him, choking on his blood with my eagerness, I let him drop and saw men and women fleeing in every direction. Did I fear that this one outrage was not a far enough step, or was my unleashing so total that I thought only of predation? Regardless, I indulged my speed and ran them down, one after another, each further from the city than the last, until there was a trail of victims behind me and I found myself alone on a little plain, with a range of nine hills ahead and a stream fat with the recent rains laughing over the rocks beside me, and full as a tick.

In the distance were barely discernible figures, dwarfed by the dust raised in their flight. I must have looked fully the monster then, my hands and face besmirched from reckless feeding and my clothes tattered where I had shown no concern for them in my frenzy. I stood for a moment in that strangely peaceful, pastoral setting and willed myself toward a modicum of control. I had come near to achieving this when I felt the tap on my elbow.

Chapter Twenty-Three

I did not have to turn to know that I had finally summoned the adversary I'd sought, but turn I did.

The creature conjured up an expression of surprise, dark eyes and pretty, bright mouth wide, and spoke in her distinctive little-girl voice.

"Oh my, pardon me! I imagined I was meeting Jinyu Liu, a poor Chinese peasant child seduced by the Red Lanterns, but surely she never had such unusual eyes!"

I studied my adversary. She seemed so small and human, surely her strength could not be as great as I feared? The warmth given off by her skin and even her faint aroma, akin to new-mown hay, bespoke humanity or something quite like it. And yet there was the aura of age, and her obvious lack of trepidation at facing me, no matter how terrible my aspect.

"It is me nonetheless, Huo," I answered, "but perhaps the time for all subterfuge is past, and you should call me Paulette Monot."

"'A rose by any other name,'" the creature replied, her voice absurdly musical, and then paused to wave her fan in front of her face as if dispelling some airborne foulness.

"But sweet you are not, little Paulette Monot. You smell of blood, and offal, with perhaps a *soupçon* of fear? What happened to the well-behaved little blood sucker I had become so fond of? Were you so very desperate for my attention?"

If the creature had her way, I believe Huo would have happily bantered until the Enclaves and Peitang fell, until the foreigners were dead one and all and the Empire doomed. Rather than engage her thusly, then, I made a final attempt at reason.

"The Dowager is preparing to leave her city, Huo, the fate of the Qing balances on the edge of a sword. You are of China, are you not? Surely you will not let this catastrophe unfold?"

The entity pranced in front of me, spinning on its pretty little feet as if accompanied by song.

"China is not the Empire, dear Paulette, which is a lesson the hag Cixi has never understood, I fear. Emperors and their families come and go, like leaves that unfurl green in spring and spill like blood on the forest floor every autumn. And still China persists. If you would whine about Empires you needs talk to a dragon. They are, I believe, more heavily invested in the families of men than am I. I say let the Qing fall, and we shall see whose head rises above the corpses next time."

"Perhaps if I begged," I said, the words burned in my throat like gall. "Would that move you to reconsider?"

"You may plead if you like, blood sucker, but what is all this to you? It is neither your land nor your fight. Your thespian Mistress will forgive your failure here, I'm quite sure of it."

"There are those I care for, whatever the reason." I continued, each word new to me as I spoke it, an unfurling lesson in the humanity I had yet to shed. "I would spare Lieutenant Henry and his beau, Belle, and even Morrison who denied me and Li-hua who cursed me." (I did not mention Miho, though my thoughts were with her too, for fear of alerting Huo to her nature, wherever she was.) "They may be as short-lived as insects, but though their flights are brief can I not at least wish them good weather?"

Huo circled me now, still dancing as it to a melody, her fan flirting all the while.

"You have been so busy, with your Imperial *tête-a-têtes*, your comings and goings into and out of the Fu, with your butchery of the populace hereabouts, that it seems you have not kept up with recent events. I, however, have seen all, and thus I will attempt to set your mind at ease."

I followed her turning, facing her all the while, as Huo continued.

"Pretty Li-hua, you see, has abandoned the Red Lanterns and serves another, converted by the kindness of the Legation doctors. She is an acolyte of the goddess of pleasure now, for which I believe she has you to thank? She exchanges her affections for privilege, and has even parlayed for herself the run of the Enclave; an advantage earned in the arms of a certain journalist, who himself is perhaps chasing the memories of another Chinese girl who need not be named."

I walked stiff-legged as we circled, tautly strung, my teeth slipping free once more. I felt my sash in vain for the lost pepper-box, though even its special bullets would likely not have aided me here.

"And it seems a cannon shell breached the barricades of the Cathedral at the end of July, and the heroic Lieutenant was among the first on the scene. Unfortunately a sharp-shooter's bullet took him through the mouth. He was able to stagger a few feet before he fell into the arms of his beloved, who had followed the troops there to provide aid. The same rifleman fired again, and so the couple perished together. It is quite amazing, is it not, how much more effective bullet and shell can be when they are no longer aimed too hi..."

I leapt at her then, her final word lost in a shriek. I felt her delicate body in my arms, and drove my mouth at her throat, planning to rip and tear until I felt the stick of her spine between my teeth.

It was not to be. There was an explosion of light, white and burning the world away. I was flung from my enemy, was rolled and tumbled across the rocks and dust, and I came to rest afire.

I understood then why the Christians imagine their hell a place of flames. There are no words to describe my pain. I would have clawed my very flesh from my bones if I thought that doing so would ease my agony even one iota. My sight was gone, my eyes long boiled away, and yet my world was red with hurting. When the final darkness opened before me I fled into it as gratefully as any child from a violent home plunges into sleep.

And then there was nothing.

Chapter Twenty-Four

The ticking was there before there was hearing, an almost aural touchstone. It was not a form of comfort, as that concept was still far distant, but only the void being given shape and border by this lonely little rhythm. Before even the word, there was the clock, the old iambic of the heartbeat calling us to consciousness.

The pain rode back in on it, as if I woke to a cymbal-crash of agony. But it was a waking nonetheless, and rising through that pain, a melody of bubbles singing up through blood, shaping the world with its ascendance, was the siren song of another's heartbeat. Imagine blood as electricity, and the fatal chair not ending something but opening a door anew. I gagged, and whimpered, and opened my new eyes.

"Sister-kin," said Miho, "how sad I would be if I had arrived too late. I had needs first to seek a guide to lead me."

She pulled her wrist from my mouth, managing to seem gentle in so doing despite the desperate scrabble of my attempts to hold it to my lips. Thus one hand was the first part of myself that I saw, and it laid the groundwork for everything I was still to understand.

My skin was pale, the white-pink of a Londoner's first seasonal foray to the beach. The me that had grown back, dragged into being by Miho's Kindred blood, showed no sign of the dyes and disguises that had so long marked me. Naked and pale, blond hair tangled over the white ridges of my shoulder bones, I heaved myself to my now bare feet.

Some distance from me, Huo, still in her girlish form, was leaning over, hands on her knees, as if chasing after breath. On some level it pleased me to see that what she had done to me had indeed cost her, but I dared not infer vulnerability from this. She had, after all, erased me whole, and without Miho's intercession there would be no tale to tell here. I turned to offer what gratitude I could in what time we both had left.

"Sister-Kin," she said again, herself clearly weakened by the draught I had needed to bring me back from the brink, "I had never thought you blond!"

I was about to respond, but noticed that Huo was once more erect, and her dark eyes flicked from one of us to the other in clear confusion.

"You live, Paulette Monot!" She said, now upright and seeming little the worse for her efforts. "And all pink and fair, too? I confess this is an outcome I had not anticipated. Even less so your companion, whose actions betray her kind, and of whom I have apparently been in ignorance."

Though she clearly knew that Huo's current form was nothing more than a whim, Miho chose to address her as if she were the Chinese girl we saw, with a lecturing air of candied condescension.

"I am Wakahisa Miho, monster," she said, with a pretty curtsey. "And you find yourself facing sister-Kin. We shall be gentle with you if you only surrender now."

Huo's image shivered, as if the illusion were too much to maintain, or had merely outlived its purpose.

"What is more to the point, maid of Nippon," she said, "is how is it that I have not detected you before? I have long kept the Middle Kingdom free of such as you. But no matter. Do you honestly believe this is the first time I have faced two such creatures at once? As I understand it there is no hell for such as you, just the suffering and then the end. You should be grateful, leaving this realm is far more difficult for other creatures, or so I hear."

As arrogant as Huo's words were, however, she did not engage in hostilities immediately, which gave Miho and me a chance to position ourselves the better to divide her attack and thus discover an opening through which to attempt her conquest. Bare feet on the stones (my nakedness of no matter to the three of us involved here), I sidestepped until Miho was opposite me and the creature in the middle.

Huo, meanwhile, muttered to herself until she was lost in a heat-haze, that illusion losing itself in a burst of flame; the black smoke following this drifted off to reveal a gigantic toad creature, at least a horse and a half high, crouching where the Chinese maiden had stood, with smoke still drifting in weak tendrils from its wide and horny mouth.

"A pair of blood-suckers," it said, still in the same singsong girl's voice, "I haven't had such a treat in just ages."

I had no thought but to follow Miho's lead, my own offensive against Huo having taught me a lesson in humility. For the moment, though, it seemed enough for my sister to continue to taunt.

"You must be wondering how I am all of a sudden here and reveled to you," she teased, "me whose invasion you had no inkling of. What if there are hundreds of us, thousands? What if we only mock you here to prolong our pleasure at your ending?"

The toad face warped, the child's voice misshaping it as it spoke; and its cheeks swelled, their color diluted, as the fire built inside.

"Two or two thousand, it matters little to me." Huo preened in her girlish tones. "You can burn, that is all I need to know. All that is carbon will fall to flame."

What a strange tableau we must have made; a dainty Japanese girl in formal kimono, a monstrous toad with a child's voice, and an Occidental woman quite bereft of clothing.

However our trio, no matter how unearthly, seemed unable to generate either astonishment or fear in the figure that then approached us. He appeared as a hermit is often depicted in folk tales; dressed in rags and proceeding haltingly with the aid of a stick, save that the fine strands of his hair and the sparse wisp of a beard that straggled from his chin were not white but an emerald blue.

Our eyes were all upon the man as he slowly made his way to within steps of the developing confrontation, there to lean upon his staff as if weary. I knew not what to make of this happenstance, but Miho's eyes shown with delight and

Huo swelled visibly, flame showing itself behind the skin of her distended neck.

"Pray forgive my intrusion," the new arrival spoke after seemingly recovering his breath. His voice was cracked and ancient, and squealed like a machine grown dry from lack of use. "But you see," he clearly addressed Huo now, "I cannot allow this maiden to be burned," his black eyes flicked toward Miho, quick as a snake's tongue. "For she has something of mine."

When Huo replied it was with the petulance of a spoiled child denied, puffs of black smoke escaping with each word.

"You dare show yourself here?" She said, anger and disbelief warring in her tones. "The dragons of China will destroy you!"

The old man clicked his tongue in disapproval and shook his head.

"They might, they might," he allowed. "But they are asleep, and slow to awaken. I believe I could just have time."

At this Huo belched a ball of fire at the sage, who despite his apparent infirmity sidestepped it easily. Even at my little distance I felt the heat of the attack, my unprotected skin briefly blistering before it could heal itself. Despite the blood I had glutted myself on earlier, and Miho's precious gift, I was aware of the weakness generated by even this healing. There was, I feared, little threat left in me.

Before the toad could strike at him again, however, the old man began a transformation of his own, and all thoughts of my own abilities were washed away with wonder.

Like the fireworks children call black snakes, which when lit rise and twist into serpents of ash; or like a vine twisting up from a single pea, were that miracle accelerated into the work of a moment; he seemed to crawl up out of himself, as blue-green as his hair had been, writhing and twining until some ten yards long, as thick as an ox in the chest and tapering into a tail that looked as delicate as that of a kite. With tiny wings and four legs that almost appeared vestigial, and a fox-faced, long antlered head set with great ruby eyes, the thing's length seemed in constant motion, twisting and snarling as if it would tie itself in knots, and rippled blue as a still harbor brushed by breeze. Here was my first dragon.

"Your arrival is most welcome here, Watatsumi-san," said Miho with a little bow.

"I had no choice, child," the dragon spoke, its voice alone unchanged, though with a scolding edge to it. "You have put that which I gave you in jeopardy, and I cannot allow our demon here to touch it."

"You fool, the beasts of China come," screamed Huo, "to finish whatever is left of you when I am through." Swelling like a balloon, she threw another great burp of flame directly at the dragon, more terrible even that her first attack.

Watatsumi raised its head like a cobra, and answered with a stream of water blown from its gaped mouth, meeting the fire midway between them in a billow of steam.

Thus they struggled, the dragon taking to the air, tiny wings blurred as a hummingbird's, and long body twisting like a scarf thrown by a gale; the toad squat and immobile. The air around us was soon thick with steam, and the battle could only be viewed in fits and starts as the white billows rose and dissipated.

They seemed evenly matched, fire and water each nullifying the other. As the creatures struggled I felt the ground roll beneath me, rising like an ocean wave. My first thought was earthquake, a disaster which this country is often tormented by, but a glance behind me showed that the range of nine hills there had grown steeper and more pointed with each shrug of the earth.

"A Chinese dragon arises, Watatsumi," screamed Miho, perhaps unnecessarily.

In reply the blue serpent attacked with more vigor, its plumes of water pushing ever closer to Huo as they drove the flames back, but as we watched those streams grew steadily smaller, as if its reservoir were running dry.

Huo noticed this as well, and redoubled her own attacks, the heat of them singing my eyebrows and now momentarily forcing the dragon to retreat.

"The tail!" Cried Miho. "Jinyu Liu, you must help me!"

I knew not what she intended, but followed her as she rushed to grasp the writhing azure snake that was Watatsumi at its thinnest point. Even this was ungodly strong, and we were flung and dragged as we grasped it, our skin breaking upon stones. I perceived Miho's goal now, however, and though we were constantly battered by the great muscle of tail, we made progress, a step lost for every two taken, and finally fell with arms full of scale into the brown waters of the swollen stream.

Watatsumi reared up as its tail was submerged, and blew a great gout of water at its enemy. Huo belched fire again and again, but the liquid attack was relentless now; finally, as the toad drew breath for yet another strike, she took a flood of water directly into her open mouth. There was a great bloom of steam, and when this drifted away Huo was nowhere to be seen.

Chapter Twenty-Five

The ground was moving constantly now, and I found it difficult to remain on my feet. To one side a foothill seemed to shrug, and I thought I could see in it a great head, yellow as dried earth and itself fully as long as Watatsumi's body, shaking itself into shape.

The blue dragon turned to Miho, and allowed a trace of smugness to creep into its ancient voice.

"It is done, child," it said, "and we must move quickly. You and I will not be welcomed here."

Miho rushed to me and took my hands in hers.

"I have done what I can, my sister-Kin. I believe we will meet again. You have won, your mission is a success. Please don't worry about me, my Masters will forget their disappointment in time, and time is a coin I can quite afford to spend."

She wrapped herself about Watatsumi's body then, arms and legs locked tight , and the dragon flung itself into the air, not so much flying but twining through it as an eel crawls up a river. In moments they were lost to sight.

Another tremor dumped me unceremoniously on my naked bottom, and when I looked up the great yellow beast shrugged itself free of the earth and regarded me and the scorched and water-soaked plain around me with blinking eyes, each the size of an ornamental koi pool in a manicured household garden.

It sniffed as if tasting the air, glanced once in the direction of Watatsumi's flight, and grumbled into speech, its voice like thunder and seeming to shake the very air around me with such force that, were I not already seated, the sound itself might have been enough to topple me.

"There has been a disturbance, yes. But it is no more." It said, sniffing again, air drawn into its nostrils with the roar of a passing train.

"It seems that Huo is gone. Ah well, she will not be missed. And the Empire survives. Nothing to keep me from napping, I see." The huge eyes blinked heavily, as if eager to remain closed, but they reluctantly opened again and took a moment to study me. I prepared to flee, knowing as I did so that the effort would be futile.

"But you, little creature," the great beast rumbled. "You should not be here. Clothe yourself and go, and pray that you never disturb my rest again."

I nodded, afraid to speak, and the dragon seemed to take that as enough. Its eyes closed, and the monstrous body twisted and shrugged, like a cat searching for comfort in a tangle of blanket. The earth heaved again, rocks fell and dust rose all around, yellowing the sun. When all this had subsided the hills were hills once more, and I was alone and naked upon the ancient earth of China.

Chapter Twenty-Six

There were clothes enough among my earlier victims to cover me, and though my skin and hair now clearly marked me as alien, I was also freed of the self-imposed meekness that had supported my disguise. Few challenged me, and those that did regretted it only briefly. A looter encountered upon the road fell to the enchantment of my eyes and gifted me with a substantial bag of silver *taels*, and by the time I arrived in Kingdow I was decently dressed and wealthy enough to procure my passage back to London.

The journey offered little in the way of new experiences, save the news that filtered to me of the relief of the Delegations by a multinational force marched through crippling heat from Tientsin. In Pekin the Western leaders found Cixi's appointed grandee to be agreeably respectful and ready to negotiate, and though those discussions would be lengthy and the punishment meted out to the Qing cruel, it appeared that, as the Chinese dragon had somehow understood, the Empire would survive.

Of course I was without my Tessier-Ashpool recording device, it and all of my other belongings having been lost when I was banished to the Fu following my trial. So I spent much of the trip dragging facts free of my cluttered memory and committing them to paper, in order to bring this account to a satisfactory close. It proved an efficient way to speed the passage of time, and in short order I found myself disembarking from the peerless *Boadicea* and once more setting foot upon the soil, or rather the pavement, of old England.

Once there, it was easy enough to convert my remaining silver into a Modern Currency, and to then purchase more appropriate attire and establish myself in a decent hotel. Thus bathed, dressed, and with Jinyu Liu only a fading memory, I presented myself to Lady Ellen.

From her I learned that my recording coils had been delivered to her address, some Samaritan apparently finding the package among Belle's belongings and completing the task she had pledged to accomplish.

The Lady was both gracious and grateful, and listened to my tale with many a satisfactory exclamation of surprise, wonder, and fright.

We talked well into the evening, and as our conversation progressed I found myself dwelling more and more on the superstitions of men, both Chinese and Western, and the fertile soil that these created, in which war could so readily take root.

Before I took my leave, the Great Actress seized my hands in hers and undertook a thorough study of my features. Once captured by her deep gaze, I could not will myself to look away, but lost myself in those peerless grey eyes; orbs that, were she bereft of limb and voice, could, I believe, have alone brought life to the most complicated creations of the playwright's art.

"You are changed, my pretty Paulette," she finally spoke. "and I find it suits you well."

I blushed at this, and for once made no effort to control my high color. Her compliment was more reward than I could have asked, though at the time I was too overwhelmed to attempt to delve into its meaning.

I was once again well paid for my adventure, but as the days have passed I've come to wonder whether my recognition of the dangers of blind faith was not the main prize that I won as a result of my efforts in the Middle Kingdom.

I wondered, too, if my achieving such a realization had been the true objective of Ellen Terry's mission all along.

On the mighty Steamship that carried me home, pleasantly sated following a dalliance with a young tourist who shared the journey, I lingered upon the deck (for we Kin are not so incapacitated by sea travel as Fiction would have us) and lost myself in reverie beneath the clot of stars only seen in skies undimmed by city lights. There I found myself speculating that growth is measured not so much in what one gains as in what one loses.

The mortal girl who was Paulette Monot, she who had cried at her transformation, was, I determined, all but lost to me; with bits of her left in the wilds of Rhodesia and more still on the scorched earth of China; the creature she was becoming has grown stronger, and more terrible, with that passing.

Even strong enough, perhaps, to face a world more terrible than she?

THE END

About the Author

Bruce Woods

Bruce Woods is a professional writer/editor with more than 30 years in magazine publishing, having worked as editor of *Mother Earth News* and *Alaska Magazine*, among others, and has published both nonfiction and poetry books. *Prairie Schooner* magazine featured his work in its "Writing from Alaska" issue. His *Birdhouse Book*, brought out by Sterling/Lark, is still in print and has sold more than 100,000 copies.

After leaving the editor's position at *Alaska Magazine* in late 1998, Woods began a second career in External Affairs for the Alaska Region of the U.S. Fish and Wildlife Service. Eventually serving as the de facto writer/editor for the agency's largest region, as well as providing information and an initial contact point for state, national, and international media on topics affecting Alaska's often controversial wildlife and land management issues, Woods retired in the spring of 2013 in order to focus on fiction writing.

His *Hearts of Darkness* trilogy, the first two volumes of which, *Royal Blood* and *Dragon Blood,* are scheduled for publication by Penmore Press in 2019.

In addition to the *Birdhouse Book* referenced above, Woods has published three nonfiction volumes and several books of poetry with small presses. During his magazine editing career he also served as editor/contributor to numerous nonfiction volumes. Several of his essays have been anthologized, as well.

Woods currently lives in Anchorage, Alaska with his wife Mary and his two cats, Lucy Fur and Boswell. Gardening and bicycling (the latter usually upon a single-speed road bike named "Yellow Snow" that he built from an old track frame bought online) are chief among his many interests outside of reading and writing. He has two children, Ethan, who studied music composition at Bennington College and now resides in Asheville, N.C., and his daughter Alice, who recently graduated from Minneapolis College of Art and Design and currently lives in Minneapolis.

ROYAL BLOOD

by

Bruce Woods

Historical and fictional characters come together and change the future of Africa forever. Renowned actress Lady Ellen Terry, detective Sherlock Holmes, financier Cecil Rhodes, hunter/naturalist Frederick Courtney Selous, King Lobengula, and a mysterious, undead adventuress named Paulette Monot become chess pieces in the Great Game, which takes the form of Africa's First Matabele War.

"It is unlikely that anyone will ever read this. In fact, if you are perusing these pages, and you're not one of the Kin ("vampires" to the uninitiated), it is almost certain that there's either been some sort of terrible mistake or that I (Miss Paulette Monot) have decided to take a mortal lover. The latter is perhaps more likely. Lucky you."

penmorepress.com

The Chosen Man

by

J. G. Harlond

From the bulb of a rare flower bloom ambition and scandal

Rome, 1635: As Flanders braces for another long year of war, a Spanish count presents the Vatican with a means of disrupting the Dutch rebels' booming economy. His plan is brilliant. They just need the right man to implement it.

They choose Ludovico da Portovenere, a charismatic spice and silk merchant. Intrigued by the Vatican's proposal—and hungry for profit—Ludo sets off for Amsterdam to sow greed and venture capitalism for a disastrous harvest, hampered by a timid English priest sent from Rome, accompanied by a quick-witted young admirer he will use as a spy, and bothered by the memory of the beautiful young lady he refused to take with him.

Set in a world of international politics and domestic intrigue, *The Chosen Man* spins an engrossing tale about the Dutch financial scandal known as tulip mania—and how decisions made in high places can have terrible repercussions on innocent lives.

PENMORE PRESS
www.penmorepress.com